GRIM INCARCERATION

ALEX BLAKE

TO MY MOTHER AND FATHER WHOM GAVE ME AN AMAZING CHILDHOOD WHICH LED TO RAISING THREE AMAZING SONS.

PROLOGUE:

Dr. Betty Reaper is a University of Kentucky house physician as well as an instructor at the neighboring Case Western Reserve medical school in which she continues to teach a few days a month. As the end of her career approaches, she decides to begin a new career path as a prison physician full time with an office located in the infirmary. Sudden deaths begin to occur at the prison along with organ theft which is discovered at the funeral parlor prior to embalming. With the help of the FBI, she has to find justice for the inmates she took an oath to protect.

Chapter 1

I began my career as a nurse in a few reputable hospitals while raising my three sons. Then following my heart to the call of a physician as they were graduating high school and following their own career paths. As a physician, I always felt there was more I could do for the prison community. After all, they deserve good healthcare while serving short term, life or even death sentences. Physicians take an oath to give the utmost of care without judgment. First day on the job, two guards roll through the infirmary door with a prisoner gasping for air while clutching his chest. Captain Jake Sigler and his brother Sergeant John are veteran prison guards. John says with a disgusted look on his face," Hey Doc G! This scumbag claims he is having chest pain in which I think is some bullshit to get attention but you are the boss!" Jake gives him a stern look of dismay and apologizes with a smile towards me. I begin my examination immediately and administer chest pain protocols in place for this facility. Thirty minutes later I inform them that Inmate Zigley is stable at this time but I will be keeping him in the infirmary for twenty four hours for observation. I ask Jake and John to come to my office before exiting back to their posts. Jake has a stern broad jaw with broad shoulders with the height of a giant. Blonde hair and green eyes that are kind at the moment but has the deep old soul stare as he glared at John for his disrespectful slur towards Inmate Zigley. John has a strong jaw line and broad shouldered and almost as tall as his brother. Black hair and crystal blue eyes that just glisten with mischief. Jake and John please take a seat and allow me to introduce myself as well as learn a little background of the guards that I will be working with. John quipped," I am Sergeant John Sigler! Nice to meet you Dr. G!" Jake elbowed him while introducing himself, " I am captain Jake Sigler and anything I can assist you with please never hesitate to ask Ma'am." John is wincing from the elbowing he received and rubbing his arm. Nice to meet you both and I assume you are brothers? "Yes Ma'am," they both replied simultaneously. John, may I ask why you refer to me as Dr. G? He replies with a Cheshire cat grin," Grim Reaper! Get it? He chuckles as he is apologizing. I am sorry if that offended you but it just slipped out Ma'am." I kept my glance stern as long as I could but a smile broke loose as John was beginning to look tense while apologizing. Well! You did not offend me this time but you won't get off so easy next time as I smiles at him. “Ma’am, yes Ma’am!”, John said. If you both ever need anything please never hesitate to ask me as well. It was nice meeting you both and I will let Warden Andrew know I met you. “thank you Ma’am”, Jake replied as he and John exited my office. As the guards exit the infirmary door, an attractive woman that beams with a radiant smile enters the infirmary . Tall brunette with glowing tanned skin and velvet brown eyes dressed in white starched scrubs proceeds to knock on my office door. She extends her hand as she introduces herself,” Hello Dr. Reaper. I am Claudia Kirsh and I am your new nurse hired by Warden Andrew. I am available to work any shift you deem necessary to assist in caring for your inmates” Hello to you Nurse Claudia. I am pleased to meet you. Warden Andrew hired me as well as I smiled and chuckled. Let’s hope he knows what he is doing as we begin to laugh together. Please call me Betty and please take a seat so we can get to know each other better. I see an envelope on my desk with Nurse Claudia’s name on it from Warden Andrew. As I open it to find a resume inside I let her know that I am going to refer to it as we have our discussion. Please tell me a little about yourself Nurse Claudia. With a smile and voice similar to the actress Kathleen Turner,” I have been a nurse for twenty five years in several local hospitals as I have been a resident of Grayson all of my life. I am married and have two daughters, Beth and Abbigail. Beth is married with a daughter Emilee and a step son Hayden. Abbigail is newly engaged to a woman as special as she is, Dominique. This is the first prison I have ever worked in. I am looking forward to the new career path." I was a nurse for ten years before I attended medical school right after my third son graduated high school. I am married to a retired Rear Admiral in the United States Navy. Let me show you where to clock in and if you would like to assist me with assessing Inmate Zigley that is here for observation for chest pain. He was brought to me this morning by two guards which is our facility protocol. All inmates are transported by two guards at all times throughout the prison and upon exiting for any appointments. Nurse Claudia replies," his assessment is within normal limits with no further complaints of chest pain since his arrival. I read in his chart that he has a history of hypertension which he currently receives a beta blocker twice daily. Would you like me to chart my findings?" Yes and I will show you the filing cabinet where I store current inmates that I am seeing this week then after I discharge them my files are sent to Warden Andrew's office and his secretary will place the file into the storage office which I will show you where that is as well as introduce you to Warden Andrew's legal team here on the premises. We also have a retired Judge and a social worker on staff. Though I am limited with standard infirmary medications, I do have an IVAC pump and an older model twelve lead ekg machine for inmates I can treat on the premises. I will send them to the hospital if deemed necessary. I require a phone call on all inmates brought into the infirmary no matter how minor the situation is then I will let the staff nurse on duty which protocol measure to use. I will trust your judgment to send an inmate to the hospital with a phone call to me as soon as the inmate is transported out. I have to document every transfer out of the prison no matter how minor or serious for the state prison authorities. Warden Andrew has a budget meeting monthly and we also go over the inmate transport roster in which every inmate transport has to be documented. Nurse Claudia asks," Does all staff have to attend the monthly budget meetings?' No. I have biweekly meetings with my infirmary staff which includes yours truly, Nurse Marthagail and now you my dear. Nurse Marthagail works primarily afternoon shift and I cover dayshift. I will need you for midnight shift. Is that suitable for you? "Yes. I have always worked night shift and my husband works dayshift." she replied with that sexy gruff voice. Shall we di into policies and procedures Nurse Claudia and as we go through the ever so boring material we can compare stories from our illustrious careers in the medical field. We both laugh as we drink coffee before sitting at my desk with the policy ad procedure book that is as heavy as a set of encyclopedias. Claudia begins, " I met two very handsome guards upon my arrival to the infirmary." Their names are Captain Jake Sigler and Sergeant John Sigler and before you ask, yes they are brothers. Jake is stern and has a serious look on his face but don't let that look fool you. He is very kind unless an inmate gets disrespectful or unruly, then he is a big grizzly bear. John is a jokester which his humor is much neded in this environment which can get depressing if you let it. When I first met him he called me Dr. G as he laughed and when I asked him what he meant, he laughed much harder and said Grim Reaper. He thought he offended me but he didn't. I actually found that very amusing. "That is very amusing", she said as she laughed. He knows how humorous he is too. With the inmates he is very professional but jokes with them also. They really enjoy him when he is on duty. Jake though he struts like he is full of arrogance, he is stern with the inmates. He is attentive with each inmate individually and honors their requests for supplies when asked with courtesy. We have several female guards on staff which I find very professional and they have as much strength and stamina as the males. You will meet all of the guards when you go to the cafeteria and I can say we have a palliative cuisine for a state run prison. I am friends with Guard Caroline Hurley and Guard Shelley Tedesca and we meet for lunch and evening drinks on occasion. Once you get to know us maybe you will find time to join us. “ I would love to join you all for ladies night! Thank you for that offer as I don’t have many friends to mingle with working night shift,” she replied. The mutual respect of our entire staff is quite astonishing for a prison environment. I think you will get along with everyone as I do. “ I will acquaint myself with the staff each time I work. I have worked at Grayson Memorial Hospital for fifteen years and St. Claire’s Hospital for ten years prior. I like to float the entire hospital to keep my skills up to date but emergency department has always been my specialty,” she said with pride. You will meet Nurse Marthagail if you are here until 1430. She is a veteran nurse of over forty years. She has many years of hospital experience and has worked at the Veterans Affairs clinic for ten years before coming on staff here. She has been here five years now. You are welcomed to accompany her on afternoon shift. “ I would like that very much. I can pick up dayshift as well as afternoon shift or dayshift if you ever need me to cover for you,” she replied with enthusiasm. That is great to know and I really appreciate your offer! We have a close knit team and you are going to be a nice addition Nurse Claudia. You will have the pleasure of meeting Nurse Marthagail's husband soon enough. His name is Lamar and he is our prison shuttle transport driver as well as prisoner transport to court appointments. He will tell you his whole life story in one breath. He is a southern gentleman with sweet southern charm to boot. His stories are very funny in which I make time to listen every chance I get. He was a deputy sheriff as well as an ambulance driver right here in Moorehead County. He and Nurse Marthagail have southern drawls but his is more prominent. She is pure southern sophistication with an amazing sense of humor. She is tall and slender with silver hair and brown eyes with flecks of copper. Lamar is tall with broad shoulders and built like a football player. He had black hair until he started shaving his head bald. Deep green eyes and a smile that will melt your heart. His laugh is so contagious anyone within ear shot laughs with him. When he stops by to visit, Nurse Marthagail chases him away. Though she adores the man, she laughs and says she needs a break from him at home. They argue like attorneys in court which I find very entertaining. There are so many different personalities here and hopefully you will find much enjoyment when you witness them for yourself. We deal with a sad and dismal environment but the personalities of all the staff makes a calming affect for the inmates. The inmates are generally calm and easygoing mixed with the few catawampus inmates that just can't help themselves causing a ruckus now and then. If you ever need to vent out your frustrations, please don't hesitate to request a private conversation. This environment takes some getting used to at times. " I will adapt pretty quickly Doc and I will take you up on that compassionate offer," she said with appreciation. Nurse Marthagail asked me recently if she could work twelve hour shifts three days a week. Would you be interested in that schedule as well? I will have to ask Warden Andrew to hire another nurse part time if not. The shifts will be 1500-0300 and 0300-1500 three days a week. I cover all dayshifts and I can cover the extra twelve hour shift but if that becomes too much I will definitely need a part time nurse but I will trial this schedule then send the request to Warden Andrew after our next monthly budget meeting. "That will definitely work for me'" she said.

I teach at Case Western Reserve medical school pre-med Tuesday's and Thursday's from 1700-2100. Anatomy and Physiology with lab. Cadavers are donated to the science department by people that are wonderfully generous to do so. Nurse Marthagail as well as myself are good at covering shifts on a whim. We totally understand family emergencies better than most people. I do spend a great amount of time in my office on quarterly reports and budget reports which cannot be put aside as we are a federal and state run facility. Our budget is under constant scrutiny which is completely understandable. Warden Andrew is a very kind and humorous man until we get a surprise audit, then he is a grizly bear. He is tall and slender with broad shoulders and occasionally boasts of his height at six foot five. He has black hair and velvet brown eyes, a little pale and a smile that will melt your heart. He has a great sense of humor and I have witnessed him giving John a run for his money. His stance makes him look very intimidating but he is a teddy bear. The inmates respect him as he respects them. All of our staff honestly appreciates and admires him for the hard work he does to ever change the prison policies to accommodate the inmates. He is a true advocate for them in which he gets nothing but repect from anyone who has encountered him in action. Meetings with al of the department heads are very entertain. Captain Jake, Sergeant John and Warden Andrew are crazy funny when they are together in the same room. You would honestly think they are related! Warden Andrew always begins his meetings with an epilogue. "Don't bring your baggage from home nor take it home from here.

We need humor and grace to break up the monotony and the inmates sense that negativity which can get bad very quickly." Sergeant Caroline Hurley stops by occasionally and I look forward to her enlightening charismatic personality that lights up a room. She is five foot three and one hundred twenty pounds of pure toughness. She is a fifteen year veteran guard and was quickly promoted up the ranks within the first five years she was hired here. She has a refreshing soul and finds positive and upbeat humor no matter how bad the situation. She has raven black hair and deep brown eyes that glisten every time she smiles. Pale skinned beauty that could be envious. I witnessed her take down three inmates during a ruckus in the cafeteria with three swift kicks. She had them on the floor and cuffed within ten minutes time. Our guards response time is very quick which needs to be to divert a possible riot at any given moment. Warden Andrew Joseph stops by with his entourage occasionally after lunch before returning back to his office. His "dream team" as he refers to them all. Judge Nancy Consiglia is retired but consults here one day a week. Anthony Tedesca is our social worker, Todd Tedesca is our attorney and his wife Chrissy is wardens legal secretary. Guard Shelley Tedesca is their sister and Judge Nancy is their amazing mother. Shelley's son Connor is currently in law school and interns here one day a week with

Todd. They are hired on under private contracts federally but belong to our facility first. My husband stops by occasionally with lunch because he knows I get so busy I forget to eat and he frowns upon my protein bars as a permanent lunch replacement. He arrives in uniform once in a while to show off and honestly I don't blame him. His illustrious career in the Navy after only thirty years he retired as Rear Admiral. Michael Tedesca is related to wardens dream team as well. We are so proud of his military service. 'Wow! That is totally impressive Docile look forward to meeting everyone!" she said with shock and admiration. They will all be happy to meet you as well Nurse Claudia and I believe you will acclimate very quickly with the staff and inmates. Well hello Nurse Marthagail! Meet Nurse Claudia Kirsh. She is our new nurse and if you don't mind she would like to train with you for a few days. " Well hello to you both and very nice to meet you Nurse Claudia! You are very welcomed to join me as I would love the company." she replied with her sweet southern drawl. I will leave you both to get acquainted as I have a few errands to run on my way home today. Thank you Nurse Claudia for the great conversation as you will be a great addition to our team. "It was my pleasure Doc! Thank you for the very educational training day," she replied with that radiant smile. Goodnight Nurse's and please don't hesitate to call me with any questions or concerns. "Good night Doc!", they both said simultaneously. Nurse Claudia calls me at 1600 to ask if she can begin her shift at 0300 instead of beginning the following day as scheduled. I was relieved to be able to begin my work day at 0800 instead of covering night shift myself. I jolt awake to the phone ringing at 0400. Nurse Claudia requests with a slight panic," I am sorry to bother you Doc but at 0230 Nurse Marthagail and I were assessing Inmate Zigley before she clocked out but he was unresponsive. We coded him for twenty minutes without success!" I will be there within the hour and I will call his family and the county coroner. Nurse Claudia asked with a slight hesitation," The county coroner?" Yes. Anytime there is a sudden death, it is policy to call him in to evaluate the patient, release his complete medical chart then he will sign the death certificate and release form to the chosen funeral parlor. When I arrive to the infirmary, Nurse Claudia has a look of distraught as Nurse Marthagail is charting final notes on the computer. I ask them to give me a report from the moment they assessed Inmate Zigley for my report. Nurse Claudia begins with a soft voice," We assessed him together and I called an ambulance while Nurse Marthagail began cpr and I grabbed the AED and attached the defibrillator pads. He had no cardiac rhythm nor respirations. I followed the instructions from the AED and he was shocked three times without any signs of life. The ambulance arrived and the paramedics took over cpr." Nurse Marthagail adds," I assessed him right before I left the infirmary for my fifteen minute break and his vital signs were stable with no complaints all shift. He verbalized that he felt good and was resting comfortably until he was awoken for my end of shift assessment. The paramedics called Dr. Jay Sutton, MD and reported their assessment with time of death. He said he was coming in and he is aware that you were on your way in as well."

CHAPTER 2

Nurse Marthagail, you and Nurse Claudia look over your charting and you can go home. Claudia can assist me with printing out his medical records for Dr. Sutton as I have the guards gather his personal belongings from his cell for his daughter

Brittany Faith to pick up when she comes in to sign discharge and release forms for Stattin -Baraski funeral parlor to pick up his body. I will call Steve and give him notification before Andrew Zigley's daughter arrives so he will have an estimated time to arrive. Nurse Claudia says," I didn't see any family or emergency contact information in his file. How did you know he had a daughter or had a preference in place for a funeral parlor?" All of that information is kept in the inmates files in the wardens office. I am aware of each and every inmates preferences in an emergency, their family contacts and their choices of funeral services upon their demise. I will show you the next day you train with me which is Friday. I will call his daughter while we wait for Dr. Sutton to arrive and you can call the guards to bring his personal belongings to the infirmary. The guards can transport him to the basement where the morgue is located after Dr. Sutton finishes his assessment. " We have a morgue in the basement?' Nurse Claudia asked with surprise. Yes. A small morgue with a 2 bay freezer. I have a small lab with phlebotomy supplies and an autopsy table. I haven't used it for a few years. Dr. Sutton and I teamed up after a riot broke out two years ago that resulted in two deaths. His morgue was occupied with five bodies to be autopsied from a bus accident. I assist him at the Grayson County Morgue occasionally upon his request for multiple deaths. We attended medical school together and he is also one of many colleagues I teach with at Case Western Reserve Medical School. “Wow! That is very interesting Doc!” Claudia replied. He also has a very impressive general practice located in Moorehead County. I honestly don’t know how he has time to do half the tasks he does very successfully but he does without ever complaining. He is six feet tall, slender build, sandy blonde hair beginning to silver at the temples and crystal blue eyes. Don’t let his stern expression fool you. He has a great sense of humor with an old fashioned bedside manner that is praised by each and every patient he encounters. I have only seen him unsettled once in my career when I assisted him with autopsies of a family of five with three small children after a house fire three years ago. “I am sorry I have to meet him with this situation but eager too all the same,” Claudia replied with a low tone. Dr. Sutton arrives to the infirmary and says,” How is my favorite Doc doing this fine morning?” I am just peachy my favorite Doc as we laugh together. I would like you to meet my newest addition to the infirmary, Nurse Claudia Kirsh. “ Well, very nice to meet you Nurse Kirsh’” he replied with a charming deep voice. “ I am pleased to meet you as well Dr. Sutton and please call me Claudia,” she replied with her deep sexy voice. He smiled at her and asked,” You look very familiar Claudia. Have you worked locally before aspiring this rewarding transition?" " I have worked at Grayson County Hospital as well as Moorehead County General for twenty years combined," she replied with a return radiant smile. " That's where I have seen you before. I never forget a pretty face'" he replied with a boyish grin. Well, shall we get started Doc flirt? We all laugh together. "My assessment is complete and I see no reason why the funeral parlor can't pick his body up as soon as they can. I have his file in which I will dictate my findings at the morgue. The guards can transport him to the morgue whenever you give the word Boss Doc," he replied with the same boyish grin. Oh1 You stop that mister comedian! Always the funny man when the time is right as usual. " It was nice meeting you Dr. Sutton instead of in passing as you recall," Claudia said with a now prominent soothed voice. I will call the guards for transport and Brittany Faith to let her know she can arrive at her convenience. The guards enter the infirmary with Inmate Sparkz in a wheelchair as he is slumped over. "Sorry Doc. G! Guard Jimmy Williams and I were on our way down, when I saw Inmate Sparkz on the floor of his cell with drool on his chin. I had Jimmy grab the wheelchair and here we are! Two birds with one stone huh?" John quipped with his usual sick humor. As John and Jim are assisting Inmate Sparkz onto the gurney I ask Nurse Claudia to assist me with the evaluation and assessment of Inmate Sparkz. Nurse Claudia will you please get a blood glucose reading as I perform my physical assessment? “Certainly Doc,” she replied. Andrew, can you tell me how you feel and when you became ill? “ “I didn’t eat my diabetic snack last night because I felt weak and nauseated. I just went to bed and when I woke up to use the urinal, I became dizzy suddenly and before I knew it here I am,” he replied with a soft weak voice. “His glucose reading is 48 Doc.” Claudia replied. Give him instant glucose gel under his tongue please and pull an ampule of glucagon and inject it now. I am going to draw some blood and send it out to the lab . I will start an IV and run 1 liter of dextrose and saline over two hours. It has been fifteen minutes since your medications were administered inmate Sparkz. How are you feeling? “ I feel a little better Doc.”he replied softly. I will repeat your blood glucose reading and order you breakfast to be delivered here. Your repeat glucose reading is ninety. I am going to keep you in the infirmary today for observation then you can return to your cell as long as your blood sugar stays within your normal guidelines. “Thank you Doc. I will nap until my tray arrives,” he said softly with appreciation. Nurse Claudia is charting on inmate Sparkz then follows me to my office. She asks, “ I am not feeling well Doc. Do you mind if I go home

/ I will get some rest and hopefully feel better to return at 0300 for my shift." Sure you can and please call me later to let me know how you are feeling so I can cover your shift. "I sure will and thank you Doc," she said with a grimace. As Nurse Claudia gathers her work bag and sweater she exit's the infirmary and instead of exiting the employee door, she clocks out and scurries to the service elevator to the basement. She enters into the morgue and as she enters John and Jim are placing Inmate Zigley into the cold storage unit. As they exit the morgue, she opens the cold storage door and rubs his chest vigorously with her knuckles known as a mid sternal rub which is painful enough to arouse an unresponsive patient when necessary. His eyes begin to open to a slit. She grabs a ventilator from the storage unit and hooks him up toot in a hurry. She thinks to herself," I have to hurry before the tetrodotoxin wears off. She puts on a gown and dons gloves and proceeds to choose a scalple. She quickly turns him to his side and extracts his right kidney then sutures his incision closed with great precision. She was employed with life banc organ harvesting in her past but did not add it to her resume. She removes him from the ventilator then smothers him with a pillow. She puts the ventilator into the storage closet and covers it with a tarp. She whispers into his ear as she places his body back into the cold storage unit,"

My friend, your donation is going to save a life." Claudia sneaks out of the morgue bay doors and reaches her car to then exhale with a smile as she looks into the rearview mirror. Nurse Marthagail arrives as I am finishing up my charting on Inmate Sparkz. She says with a smile," How ya doin Doc and where is Nurse Claudia?" She went home a few hours ago voicing she wasn't feeling well and said she will call me later with an update so I will know if I need to cover her shift. I am very tired my dear and thank you for asking. "sure thang Doc. I worry about you workin so many dang hours. I can't believe how quickly Inmate Zigley crashed on us really. I hate to talk ill about anybody and as sweet as Claudia is, I just get a bad vibe with her and maybe it's my paranoid thinking but my vibes are neva wrong, she replied with that sweet southern drawl I love to hear so much. I won't hold that against you dear as I smile at her and she smiles back with her index finger pointed at me to behave myself. I don't have any gut feelings about her but I hardly know her yet. Dr. Sutton recognized her immediately from Grayson and Moorhead hospitals. "Docta Sutton knows anybody and everybody, especially if they are a pretty little thang as Nurse Claudia surely is," she said with sass. Yes. I agree with you Miss observant. He has always been a flirty charmer as long as I have known him but he is happily married and would run for the hills if another woman called him on his harmless advances. We both laugh with hysterics and I do that easily when I am tired. Let me give you report on Inmate Sparkz that came in suddenly when John and Jimmy were enroute to pick up Inmate Zigley. He was found on his cell floor drooling. His blood glucose was very low and upon diabetic hypoglycemic protocol, his blood sugar increased and with some IV fluids and lab work he has been stable. He will be staying here until morning. "Did inmate Zigley's daughter stop in and did the funeral parlor pick him up yet?" she asked. Steve called me from Statin-Baraski and informed me that he had a few pick ups before Zigley and would be arriving in an hour. He was a really respectful man. He was going to be paroled in three months after serving five years for armed robbery. "Yeah, he was very darn respectful. His Mama raised him right he just made a mistake is all. His daughta Brittany Faith is a sweet girl. She stopped by one day while visiting her daddy when I called for the guards to bring him down for a blood pressure check," she said with a smile. I met her a few times myself when I left from the main entrance one day after a budget meeting she was exiting at the same time. She thanked me for being kind when treating her father in the infirmary during his hypertensive crisis a few times before we got him regulated. Well my dear, I am heading home to take a long bubble bath then early to bed. Michael will have to fend for himself for dinner because I had a late lunch and honestly I am too damn tired to eat. Have a good shift and you know the drill…..As she laughs she says," Yes Ma'am I surely do!" I awake to a phone call from Nurse Claudia," Sorry to bother you Doc but Inmate Sparkz has taken a turn for the worst and is in a coma. I called the ambulance and they are on their way." she said with a sad tone. I look at the clock and it is 0500. I slept like I have never slept before. I will be there in twenty minutes. Have the paramedics wait for me before leaving please. " I certainly will Doc," she replied. As I enter the infirmary the paramedics are awaiting my arrival patiently. Geoffrey has been a medic for several years partnered with his wife Anna. "hey Doc! Long time no see, not!, he says with a Cheshire cat grin resembling John. Please stay while I assess Inmate Sparkz then I will inform you both of my plan. As I begin to assess him, the monitor that is attached to his chest begins to flat line. Geoffrey and Anna shock him three times accompanied by cpr over twenty minutes without success. "Doc! I am so very sorry for your loss again. We heard about Inmate Zigley from Rudy Harsan our Captain yesterday during our meeting," he said with a kind voice. Anna smiled and said, " Sorry Doc. Do you want me to call Dr. Sutton?" No honey but thanks for asking. I will call him. "Take care Doc! It is always nice to see you", Geoffrey and Anna say simultaneously. They make a very cute couple and they are wonderful paramedics. I ask Nurse Claudia to give me report as she is charting at my desk. " I had just assessed him and checked his blood glucose which was 100. He said he was feeling good and he ate two diabetic snacks as well as drank three cartons of milk at 2200 in which his blood glucose level was 130 at bedtime. When I tried to arouse him , his skin was cool and clammy and I was unable to arouse him with a sternal rub. I called the ambulance then called you." she said with a stern voice. Nurse Marthagail asked me to ask you if you could possibly come back in at noon. She has an appointment that couldn't be scheduled after her shift at 1500. "Since I am already here, why don't you go home now and get some rest. I will call Dr. Sutton then the guards for transport to the morgue. I have to call his sons and daughter as well. "I am caught up and I could use some extra rest," she said. I will catch up on my charting and budget reports after I print out reports for Dr. Sutton. Dr. Sutton arrives as quiet as a ninja and knocks on my office door which startled the be Jesus out of me. I picked up that word from Lamar our transport driver. 'I see you missed me already Doc!, he said with a chuckle. Oh yes! I miss you every second of everyday Jay, just don't tell my husband I finally admitted this. " he replied with a laugh, " ok! Right back at ya! This will be our secret from our spouses!" We both laugh together. How about a cup of coffee while I fill you in on Will Sparkz. " I never turn down a cup of coffee from a pretty lady," he boasted with that boyish grin. Yeah, yeah Jay. He arrived to the infirmary after being found laying on his cell floor with drool on his chin yesterday morning. He was weak but was able to get up and into a wheelchair with assistance. I checked his blood glucose which was very low and progressed with the hypoglycemic protocol. He was stable and after some IV fluids I decided to keep him for observation due to his brittle diabetic history. He was eating and stable until 0500. I printed his medical chart for you. I sent blood work out yesterday as well. "I will assess him and lets get some blood work. I am going to release his body to the family and the funeral parlor. " he says as he hands me the forms signed needed for prison policy. 'We really have to stop meeting this way Doc! I will be teaching with you Tuesday evening if you want to grab an early dinner before class? He asked ever so kindly. Sure Jay, that sounds good. We can chat about our medical school days when you used to get me into trouble. He laughs loudly and says," You mean you got me into trouble Missy!" "Good morning Doc," said Nurse Claudia. I can't believe it is 1130 already. I am going home soon. Inmate Sparkz's family are in the morgue paying their respects before Statin-Baraski picks him up at 1400. His wife Marge, daughter Michelle and sons Lee and Scott will stop to see you before they leave to pick up his personal affects. " I will accommodate them any way I can'" replied Claudia with a compassionate voice. The paperwork for Steve is on my desk in the file box. "I will make sure he gets it. Is there anything pertinent I need to know before you leave Doc?" she said with her million dollar smile. No. As I gathered my briefcase and jacket, the infirmary door swings open by guards Will Drost and guard Caroline Hurley with inmate Nathan Spade in a wheelchair gasping for air. Place him upon the gurney please. As I grab the pulseoximeter to read his oxygen saturation and place him on oxygen via nasal cannula. His oxygen saturation reads 89 percent. He has a history of asthma. Inmate Spade has been incarcerated for 5 years and is currently serving a ten year sentence for second degree murder. He was an accomplice during an armed bank robbery and his partner Michaela White shot the bank teller. His gun was a toy and he vehemently swore that he had no idea her weapon was authentic. Judge Nancy Consiglia ruled over his case which was her last before she retired after forty years on the bench. His attorney was Thomas Xena with a record of over two hundred wins as a top notch defense attorney. Please administer an aeresol via mask treatment over two hours and I begin a prednisone dose pack for seven days by mouth. Call Bivins Mobile x-ray and have them perform a two view chest x-ray. Draw blood work. Complete metabolic panel, complete blood count and a histamine panel as well as arterial blood gases stat. I will fill out the orders and leave them on my desk before I leave. As I try to leave once again, I assess inmate Spade's status. His oxygen saturation is 98 percent with eased respirations at this time. I ask him how he is feeling and he gives me two thumbs up while his aeresol mask is in place. Let Nurse Claudia know if you begin to experience any shortness of breath immediately Nathan. He gives me one thumb up and waves with his other hand. I am finally leaving Claudia, finally as I let out a sigh of relief. "Be safe going home Doc. I will let you know if there are any changes in his status." she replied with assurance. I will review all of is test when I come in tomorrow morning. I am also expecting lab work results from the university portal for inmate Sparkz. "Oh! Ok are you expecting any lab work from inmate Zigley as well?" she asked with an odd concern. As a matter of fact, I meant to look at the portal earlier but I will look at it in the morning and fax it to Dr. Sutton. "Have a good rest of your day Doc," she said with an impish smile. I have to go home and take a nap before teaching this evening. Honestly! What a few hectic days it has been. I would like to know what the hell is going on in my infirmary. I finally make it home throughout a long wait on interstate sixty four due to a multiple vehicle accident. Patrolman Rowley waved me through or I would have sat there for God only knows how long. Patrolman Rowley is also a paramedic whom I met five years ago while covering Grayson County General's emergency room. He is about six feet tall with a slender build. Blonde hair, cerulean blue eyes and a smile that will melt your heart. After a refreshing nap, I am ready for an exciting evening of lecturing and teaching in the medical school lab. I have always loved teaching but I enjoy the hands on work much more. As a nurse, I loved holding my patients hands and listening to their life stories. My father tells the most amazing life stories ever. His childhood consisted of rock caves, waterfalls and campfire iron skillet chow. His brother Willie once blocked him in a rock cave and went home to do his chores when my grandfather Bill asked him why he wasn't being helped by Watt, he suddenly remembered he had to run as fast as he could to release the boulders he placed in front of the cave. So many interesting and funny stories and too little time my father always says after each story.

Chapter 3

I reach the medical lecture room finally with a warm welcome from all of my students. I have one hundred medical students this year with rotation schedules in the lab that consists of twenty five students. They are so eager to learn as I always was. I learn something new everyday. I always inform my students that when your brain feels like it can't possibly absorb anything new, you finally graduate and continuously learn new life orders that will astonish and amaze you. Human nature has always amazed and astonished my psychological need to observe but the shocking experiences stays with you for much longer. After a fulfilling evening lecturing, on to the fun in the lab. As I walk into the lab, I immediately notice a very familiar cadaver. Oh my God! This is Inmate Andrew Zigley. I wasn't aware that he donated his body to science. I go into my office to look at his demographics just to make certain that my eyes aren't deceiving me. Well old friend, my students will take good care of you. As my students begin to arrive after a brief break, Paula, Sara, Hope, Danielle, Marie and Grace are assigned to Andrew. They begin autopsy procedure. They roll him over to inspect his body posterior and begin to compare his medical record to his body markings for routine surgeries he had in the past as to make sure the incision scars are all documented accurately. Grace immediately observes and thinks intuitively to herself, “An incision to the posterior right flank that is not documented anywhere in his medical record. The incision is purple and still has black sutures visible. No betadine is visible on his skin either. Sometimes post operative betadine is seen on the skin for a week or longer. I have to ask Dr. Reaper if part of the medical record is perhaps misfiles or even missing entirely.” I hear a knock on my door as I finish the medical school rotation roster for Thursday. Hello Grace. What can I assist you with as I get up from my desk. “ I have a question regarding Andrew Zigley’s file. It is missing some paperwork from a recent surgical procedure that appears to be fairly recent.” My heart begins to race because I know for a fact that he has had no recent surgical procedures within the last five years that I have cared for him at the prison. I walk towards the table with Grace and my gut begins to sour very quickly. Oh Hell to the no! I gather my composure and smile at Grace and the other girls. I tell them that their must be paper work that was left out of his file and I will look into his medical records to find it. They all smile and thank me. I ask Dr. Sutton to join me in my office immediately. Please lock he door behind you Jay as he looks at me with a big grin on his face and says," would my lady like the blinds open or closed!" Oh! Stop that silly man as I motioned for him to take a seat. " You look worried about something Miss Betty", he said with concern. I noticed Andrew Zigley donated his body to science as I entered the lab, which I had no idea he had ever considered but that is neither here nor there. That may have been a decision he made with his family and never entered it into his demographics at the prison and that is totally fine. Great even! Then Grace asks me to look into his file and retrieve a missing part of his record that consists of a recent surgical procedure the posterior right flank region with a very recent incision that still has sutures in place. His jaw dropped as he replies with concern," He has not had any surgical procedures in the last ten years. I was his general physician for the last twenty years and other than five spinal fusions and titanium cages placed to L1-L5 lumbar regions he has had no other surgical procedures." As I begin to feel nauseated, I know I have to call Steve at Statin-Baraski to inquire upon one of his technicians may be performing cadaver experimentation as a practicing medical school student might on the down low. Nurse Claudia meets with the Sparkz family and sends them on their way. She thinks to herself," I have to assess inmate Spade and hurry down to the morgue before the funeral parlor arrives. She enters the morgue and pulls inmate Sparkz from the cold storage unit. Enters the storage closet and pulls out the ventilator to set it up. Sparkz's eyelids are beginning to flutter considering he was given several doses of tetrodotoxin. Tetrodotoxin is a venom derived from puffer fish that is extremely deadly if the dosage is not carefully calculated. It puts the person it is given to into a deep coma like sleep lowering heart rate and respirations to a deceased like state. After setting up the ventilator and intubating inmate Sparkz, I don a gown and gloves along with a scalpel. Turning him upon his side I make an incision to the posterior right flank region and remove his kidney. Sewing the incision an tying the sutures in place. Then proceed to turn him onto his right side to remove his left kidney in the same manner. I remove the ventilator set up and before replacing William Sparkz back into cold storage, I smother him with a biohazard waste bag. I hurry back to the infirmary to assess inmate Spade before Steve from Statin-Baraski arrives to pick his body up. " I think to myself," I have to sit down and rest for a few minutes. I have stored the organs safely on dry ice so my daughter can stop by and pick them up soon. This place of employment is going to be unlimited for organ harvesting. Saving lives that actually deserve them will be a never ending cycle here. I should feel guilty but I sure as hell don't. These animals are incarcerated for their wrong doings and I am just fortunate to have gotten a job here to make their organs worth their forsaken sorry lives. I have to administer inmate Spades medication and aeresol treatment, As I place his aeresol mask upon his face he grimaces and his respirations become labored. I check his oxygen saturation and his numbers begin to decline rapidly. I check his oxygen line attached to the meter on the wall and it is secure. His numbers begin at ninety eight percent and within seconds drops by five increments rapidly. I call an ambulance and Dr. Reaper immediately." Hello Nurse Claudia, is everything ok? " Inmate Spade is declining quickly and the ambulance is on its way. I assessed him e few minutes ago when he went into respiratory distress and his oxygen saturation dropped very rapidly. He is unresponsive at the moment and barely breathing." she said with a stern professional voice. I am leaving the school now and should arrive in twenty minutes. As I rush into the infirmary, the paramedics Rowley and Swanson are standing at the gurney side. 'We intubated him as soon as we got here Doc! Fifteen minutes of continuous oxygenation via the ambu bag and he flat lined on the monitor in which cpr was performed without success", Swanson said with compassion. Nurse Claudia thinks to herself," tetrodotoxin works well in an aeresol inhalation technique." " Rowley asks," Doc, do you want me to call Dr. Sutton to get permission to transfer his body to the county morgue?" No thank you. I will call him myself as he has been coming here and performing his assessments before releasing the body from here if deemed appropriate. He will let me know what he wants to do after that. As the medics pack up their equipment the both say," Nice to have seen you Doc as always but not in these circumstances. "Thank you gentlemen and it is always nice to see you both as well. I can't believe this shit! Three sudden deaths in three damn days in a row! I seriously am experiencing that sickening sour stomach again but worst right now. What the hell is going on here. Warden Andrew is going to have a damn stroke as well as myself possibly! Nurse Claudia finishes her charting on inmate Spade before Dr. Sutton arrives. I will call the guards to clean out Spade's cell and deliver his personal belongings to the infirmary then call his family which I dread. I will go home after Dr. Sutton finishes his assessment in which a hot bubble bath sounds very good right now. I will call Warden Andrew as soon as I get back into my office in the morning which is another dreaded call I am not looking forward of making. The lab results on Zigley and Sparkz will have to wait to be read until morning. Dr. Sutton arrives and after his assessment, decides to have inmate Spade transported to the County morgue for autopsy. I ask him if he would like assistance and he can perform the autopsy here in our morgue. " That is a welcomed offer Miss Betty.", he said with appreciation. I will have the guards transport his body to the morgue and we can perform his autopsy together in the morning, Is that ok with you Jay? " We have had a long grueling day my long time friend. I will be here at 0800 and we can begin then," he said with a tired smile. That is a date my friend. He waved as he exited the infirmary. I am leaving now Nurse Claudia. I have supplies in the med room that need put away. Could you please do that? " Sure Doc! Anything I can do to help you." she said with a smile. I called the guards to transport inmate Spade to the morgue. I will be back at 0800. Give Nurse Marthagail a good report as you always do. " I will Doc. Be safe going home", she replied softly. Claudia thinks to herself, " I will have to hurry and extract his organs before Nurse Marthagail arrives. Beth and Mike will be here to pick them up at the morgue entrance bay. It is too risky for them to meet me here for dinner to pick them up as before. I proceed to the morgue to prep inmate Spade for organ retrieval. Should I chance extracting his heart? Beth informed me that there is a young boy on the list that is deteriorating fast. His body will be picked up in the morning by the funeral parlor so I will have to act fast so she can pick the organs up soon after. I enter the morgue right after the guards leave and scurry to pull his body from the cold storage unit and place him on the ventilator. After putting on a gown, mask and gloves, I make a Y incision and crack his ribs open to extract his heart. After pacing his heart on dry ice I close his incision then proceed to turn him from side to side to extract his kidneys bilaterally. I clean up just in time to call Beth and Mike to meet me at the morgue bay entrance then race back to the infirmary right before Nurse Marthagail arrives. Wow! I am exhausted from the last three days ! That is a lot of physical work to do alone. I really need a partner as she laughs to herself." Nurse Marthagail arrives and Nurse Claudia exit's the infirmary with a smile on her face. I arrive at 0730 and Dr. Sutton arrives just minutes later. I welcome him and offer him some coffee. Let me check the lab portal for results on inmates Zigley and Sparks then we can begin the autopsy Jay. "Sure thing. I would like to see the results as well," he said with a crooked smile. I can't believe this crazy shit Jay! I ordered a full toxicology screening on both inmates and you are not going to believe the results! Oh my God! How the hell did tetrodotoxin get into their systems? He declared in shock," I agree! What the hell is going on?" I have an emergency email from Steve the funeral director at Statin=Baraski. It reads, I noted in my initial report after picking up Andrew Zigley from your facility, he had an incision to the posterior right flank region prior to my technician even seeing him. After picking up William Sparkz, I performed his initial assessment and found the exact same incision. I chalked them up to recent surgeries and just made sure everything was documented. Sincerely, Steve. I can't believe this crazy shit, can you? "No! I have been a coroner for over ten years and I have to say yes! I remember several patients that were sent to me for mysterious sudden deaths from Grayson County General, Moorehead County General and St. Claire Medical Hospital." he said with concern. I have to call Warden Andrew then we can proceed down to the morgue. Warden Andrew has called an emergency meting scheduled for tomorrow morning. Shall we head down to the morgue kind sir? He laughs and extends his arm in jest. We enter the morgue and pull out the stainless steel table on wheels with inmate Spade's body upon it. As Dr. Sutton pulls down the sheet he gasps and his face turns red with anger as he says," Somebody already beat us to the punch Doc! Seems we weren't invited to the autopsy party!" I am now convinced that Nurse Marthagail's intuition towards Nurse Claudia was spot on. She has been with each inmate at the time of their deaths and now this. I never told her we were scheduled to do his autopsy this morning ourselves. I was so tired when I left I honestly forgot to tell her. I am certain she assumed his body would be picked up this morning by the funeral parlor. He has no immediate family except a cousin from Ohio that I spoke with last night. I'll be damned if she didn't consider that aspect! His wishes are to be cremated which are documented in his medical record. I am going to make damn sure that twisted bitch gets thrown into a dark hole for the rest of her life! "Wow Doc! I haven't seen you this angry since I vomited in your shoes after that frat party in Ohio when we visited your cousin at Ohio State University." he says as he laughs. I begin to laugh with him. "You needed to laugh a little Doc. I don't like seeing you angry my friend. Let's see what damage she left for us so I can help you nail that bitch to the wall!" he says with his charming smile. Ok, ok my sweet friend. I will call Captain Jake as soon as we are finished so he can alert his department heads of the emergency meeting scheduled in the morning. Dr. Sutton opens the fresh incisions and to our dismay, his heart and kidney's. He asks me, " Doc, please draw his blood and fluids from his liver and bladder and I will extract vitreous humor from his eyes for analysis. We are going to obtain every shred of evidence from Mr. Spade and bring him some peace when we hang the bitch for murder and organ theft." Nice Jay! We are partnered up just like we were the very first time we met at Georgetown University when I was a brief student there then transferred to University of Kentucky and you followed me. He replies with a laugh," yeah! Look at us now baby! Still friends and always will be! I will forward al of our reports to the Board of Directors at Grayson County General, Moorehead County General and St. Claire Medical Hospital to compare with their sudden death registries being that Nurse Claudia worked their during her career and just maybe we can find correlations with Zigley, Sparkz and Spade's deaths. Finding justice for them is going to be my main goal. Dr. Sutton sits on the board of directors as well as the Ethic committee's as I do. Dr. Hoffman is the president of the Ethics Committee as well as a colleague of ours. We attended Case Western Reserve Medical School with him. Dr.'s Eva Dawn and Mary Leigh are Chief's of Staff at Grayson County and Moorehead County General and their mother Martha Stella is a Professor that sits on the Ethics Committee at the University of Kentucky Hospital. I will send them an email to pull any employee records they have on Nurse Claudia Kirsh. Nurse Marthagail is sitting at my desk computer as I enter my office. "Why the serious face Doc? Did somebody run over your dog?", she says with her wiseass southern drawl that I love so much. Well my dear. I have much to tell you. I am glad you are sitting down for this. As I begin to fill her in on the past three days of shock and dismay, the phone rings. Chrissy say's, " Claudia Kirsh just called and quit her position here. Warden Andrew would like to see you right now if you could." Thank you Chrissy. I will be right up. I will be back and fill you in as I planned my dear. " I knew she would up and quit! I have had a bad feeling about her ever since I met her!, she said with a vehement demeanor. I enter Warden Andrew's office after knocking. " Please close the door and have a seat Doc. What the hell is going on? I read your email and I called the FBI to sit in on our emergency meeting in the morning. I sure hope you and Dr. Sutton have all of your ducks in a row! I am sure you do but we have to be more thorough then we have ever been regarding three damn mysterious and sudden deaths!" he said with a roar and clenched fists on his desk. I will have everything in order before I leave today. " Nurse Claudia Kirsh sure had me fooled! I usually get a gut feeling towards rotten apples but I guess I let a pretty face lead me down the wrong path," he said with an impish grin. Yeah, well, I am guilty of that myself Warden. I usually get the same gut feeling myself but not with her radiant beauty and million dollar smile. Nurse Marthagail had that eerie feeling towards her from day one but you know how she gets with her old wives tales and snaky attitude towards people. We both laugh and he says" Our very own transport driver Lamar is exactly the same cut of cloth." Southern people are very intuitive when it comes to crackpots. My grandmother's could spot a crazy person a mile away. They were known to walk a mile out of their way to avoid bad karma. Fool me once shame on me. Fool me twice will never happen. Are we finished here Warden? "yes we are Doc. Go finish your budget reports along with your meticulous medical record gathering and I will see your kind face in the morning. You have a pretty face. Are you going to lead me down the wrong path like you did for Dr. Sutton?", he boasts with his deep laugh. Oh! You better behave mister! I am laughing as I leave his office. Nurse Marthagail is sitting on the edge of her seat by the time I get back to my office. She asks with a crooked smile on her face," Well, are you going to finally tell me the juicy gossip?" You are never going to believe this crap my dear. I received the lab reports this morning and tetrodotoxin was found on Zigley's and Sparkz's toxicology panel. I forgot I ordered that test but it is standard for all of the inmates here automatically with any type of blood work or urine samples sent. The autopsy performed this morning was already initiated before we arrived on inmate Spade. Yesterday evening in the lab, I recognized Andrew

Zigley as one of the cadavers donated to the school. My student noticed during first assessment of the body before autopsy that he had a recent incision to the posterior flank region. During autopsy we discovered his right kidney was missing. Steve sent me an email and notified me upon his initial observation of William Sparkz's body, he had a recent incision to the posterior right flank region as well. He called Bivin's Mobile x-ray and I received that report this morning. His right kidney was not there. His body was transferred to Grayson County Coroners office for a full autopsy yesterday. Dr. Sutton will have his results forwarded to me sometime today. He had a rush put on lab work for Sparkz and Spade which we will need for our emergency meeting with Wardens staff tomorrow morning. Oh! The best part, he asked the FBI to step in and investigate the three tragic deaths we sadly endured in just three damn days! Nurse Marthagail's jaw is dropped as she listens then replies, "That is the most awful and craziest thing I have eva heard. I knew my intuition was dead on but I never imagined she was a killer, just sneaky and too pretty to be normal! Too pretty just ain't normal!" You are too funny my dear. We both laugh. Let's get these medial records in order. I will call the temp agency and have a nurse replace Claudia until we have Warden Andrew hire a butt ugly nurse. We both continue to laugh when

Captain Jake and Sgt. John enter the infirmary. I heard John coming up the hall with that crazy funny laugh of his. As I look up Jake blocks the entire doorway and John peeks under his arm with that impish grin of his. “Hey Doc G! You aren’t happy unless you are causing trouble now, are ya!” he said in his sarcastic funny tone.

CHAPTER 4

Jake smacks him on the top of his head and gives him his famous warning look. “ It has come to my attention that the FBI will be here for the meeting in the morning. The boy scouts are coming to our rescue no doubt.” he said with arrogance and a slight smile. “Yeah! The damn boy scouts!”, John quipped. Jake gave him a thumbs up this time. John says,” I knew that woman was too damn beautiful to be normal!” We have all come to the same conclusion, beautiful means crazier than hell! We all laugh as I inform them that I have requested the temp agency send over the ugliest nurse ever seen in history. John replies,” God no! We have enough ugly people to stare at all damn day! Please tell me you are kidding!” Jake chimes in,” OH please little

Casanova! You can't find a girlfriend outside of the prison so you want Doc to hand deliver a pretty little nurse for you to harass!" "Hell yeah boy! You read my mind as usual big brother!", John says with that Cheshire cat grin. We all laugh together. I am gathering medical records for our meeting so is that all you boys needed? We just stopped by to actually say how sorry we are regarding your losses", Jake said with kindness. John shook his head in agreement. Thank you both for stopping by. I always enjoy your visit. Not you John! As we laugh he drops his chin to his chest with a pout. As fast as he lifts his head he has that crazy look on his face and says," You'll all miss me when I am gone!" "Hell no we won't little brother!", Jake says with a big smile and elbows John in the ribs. Thanks for stopping by boy's! ok Nurse Marthagail, lets get this party started and finished so I can go home and soak in a hot bubble bath until dooms day. She replies with sass," I don't blame you one bit Doc! I sure am glad you are not crazy! As pretty as you are, you should be crazier than hell!" You better stop that! I may have to elbow you in the ribs to calm you down because it sure works for Captain Jake. We laugh together and while I print out medical records she places them ever so neatly into each designated file jacket. We are finally finished! Well Nurse Marthagail, I am out of here my dear. Thank you for all of your help and letting me vent to you. The temp agency is sending over a male nurse named David Bentley. " Oh my! John is going to have a stroke!" she said laughing so hard she was holding her stomach. I laughed so hard I though I might pee my pants. She has the same contagious laughter as Lamar. I enter the conference room and Warden Andrew is standing at the head of the table with his team at hand. As Captain Jake enters with files in hand, three FBI agents follow him to the table. Sgt. John is the last staff member to enter and says," "The most important person is here! We can get started now!" Warden Andrew gives him a stern deep stare and replies," The last person entering the room should close the door. Who stares at John and points his index finger at him. That means you John." He walks toward the door and replies," I always close the door." Jake replies," That's because you are always the last person through the door little brother." John quips." That's because I always have to finish your rounds big brother!" Warden Andrew replies," Children! Please zip it and have a seat! I say we are ready to get this meeting started and I would like Agent Alice Brubaker to introduce her team while she actually leads this meeting." She stands up and says." Good morning to you all. I am Agent Alice Brubaker and these are my team members from the task force division. This is Agent Suze Bivins, Agent Trace

Brubaker and Agent Rebecca Coy. We are here to assist you Warden Andrew Joseph and we thank you for the invitation. We have been handed files from three hospitals with over one hundred and fifty unexplained sudden deaths from the last fifteen years. When I received the phone call from Warden Andrew Joseph, I immediately looked into all of the files we have and I believe you had the main suspect we have been looking for. My team as well as myself would like to set up an office here and compare your files with ours so we can hopefully gather enough evidence to bring her ass to justice." Agent Alice Brubaker is at lets six feet tall and slender with raven black hair, cornflower blue eyes and milky satin skin. Agent Suze Bivins is five feet eight with an hour glass figure, blonde hair, crystal blue eyes of steel and skin of an Egyptian goddess. Agent Rebecca Coy stands five feet eight with auburn hair, velvet brown eyes and a milky complexion that glows. Warden Andrew adds," Dr. Betty Reaper has the inmate's files you will need and has offered her undivided attention and assistance to the agents while they are here conducting their investigation. Our facility is and staff will be happy to assist you all with anything you need as well. My assistant Chrissy has a room next door set up and Captain Jake Sigler will assist you with any other records you may need." "Thank you all again for your welcomed hospitality. My agents and I will be comfortable here and we will let you know if we need anything at all." replied Agent Alice Brubaker with her deep kind voice. I offer to show the agents to their office next door. ' Thank you Dr. Reaper and could you please stay so we can get acquainted?" I would be happy to get acquainted with you all. " could you please give us some background on Nurse Claudia Kirsh?" asked Agent Alice Brubaker. I have included her resume and background checks in a separate file for you. She told me she worked at Grayson County General, Moorehead County General and St. Claire Medical Hospitals. My colleague Dr. Jay Sutton, MD met her several times and recognized her immediately. He and I teach at Case Western Reserve Medical School and he is currently Grayson County Coroner. He is aware of your presence and has offered to assist you any way he can. I have his business card in my office and you can stop by the infirmary anytime. " I appreciate your attention and time you put in stuffing these meticulous files." she replied. I have to get some work done in my office but please don't hesitate to let our staff or myself know if we can be of any further service. As I enter my office, Nurse Marthagail is orienting Nurse David Bentley to the infirmary. She approaches my office with him and says," Hey Doc! This is Nurse David Bentley." He extends his hand and says," Hello Dr. Reaper. I am

David Bentley and I am happy to meet you." Hello Nurse David. I have read your extensive file sent over from Maximum Medical Staffing Agency and I am impressed with your work history. I am aware you have worked in several state prisons. Have you ever thought about working in one permanently full time? 'Yes Ma'am I have been considering that option lately. I am tired of floating to several different facilities and would very much like to find an employer I could call home," he replied with a smile. He stands at six feet tall with a slender build and broad shoulders. Red hair and green eyes with pale skin and about a million freckles. After you put in thirty days probationary time, I would like to meet you for an interview if that's ok with you, then we will both know if this facility will become your home employer. "He replies with a smile and soft deep voice," I would like that opportunity very much Ma'am." Good to know Nurse David. Nurse Marthagail asks him," Would you like to continue where we left off before this pretty boss blessed us with her presence?" He nods his head yes and I tell her to go away crazy lady I have work to do. She laughs as she walks towards the three bays with gurney's. As I sit at my desk to work on the quarterly budget report and my staff schedule, John enters the infirmary and knocks on my door to say," Hey Doc G! How the hell are you today? Did you hire a new pretty nurse yet?" I pointed towards the bay and as he glanced over and looked at me with a smirk. He closes my office door and sits down to say, " You are kidding me right now, right? That sure is hell is not pretty! Nor female either! He is just a temp right? Please, Please say I am right!" I have to keep my composure because I really want to laugh my face off but I will try hard not to for his poor ego's sake. I am going to interview him after working thirty days then he wants to consider working here full time if he feels comfortable enough here. "oh my God! I hope he decides not to stay on so you can hire a pretty little nurse in his place!" he voiced with a grimace and reddened cheeks. We will soon find out. "ok, ok. I have to go do rounds before Jake has a friggin cow now!, he said with that Cheshire cat grin he is so famous for which usually means he is about to cause some trouble. I will see you later John. He stands up and points at Nurse David as he walks out the door and shakes his head no vigorously. I barely wait for him to exit the infirmary door before I start laughing uncontrollably which reminds me I need to laugh more often. My office phone rings from Captain Jakes extension. Hello Jake how are you today? He replies, " Agent Alice Brubaker called me a few minutes ago and requested any video logs we have throughout the prison covering Nurse Claudia's day's here. I just viewed them and you are not going to believe what

I found Doc!" he replies with a stern voice. What did you find? He replies," She is on the tape from the morgue bay entrance with a cooler in her hand and handing it through a window of a black panel van three nights in a row. I have tried to zoom in to identify the driver and the license plate but I have not been able to do so. I will turn them over to Agent Alice Brubaker and maybe their IT department can do something with them." Wow! I can't believe how bold she was and thought she could get away from the cameras. " Sgt. Ray Kirsh was seen at the morgue bay by our transport driver Lamar several times last week. Lamar stops in my office to chat once in a while and man! That man is hilarious but very long winded! He mentioned that he saw him and stopped to ask if he was expecting an ambulance or delivery and he said he was just taking a break in peace. I am going to call him in for some questions as soon as he gets here this afternoon," he said with a stern voice. " Laughing as he hangs up, "That Lamar is a hoot!" I laugh to myself in agreement. That man would make a dog laugh. As I work at my desk filing necessary paperwork and sort the incoming mail, the infirmary doors swing open with Guard Jimmy and Guard Robin pushing inmate Brown in a wheelchair. Grasping his chest, diaphoretic and gasping for air. Nurse Marthagail and Nurse David rush over to the gurney to assist him up and onto the gurney. I get up from my chair to assist them. I thank the guards for bringing him in and the wave as they exit the infirmary. I immediately place oxygen via nasal cannula on inmate Brown and check his oxygen saturation with the pulseoximeter. The reading is eighty six percent, blood pressure one hundred seventy over ninety eight and respirations twenty six. I assess his breath sounds while Nurse David applies leads to perform and ekg. I ask Nurse Marthagail to start an IV site while I administer nitroglycerin. Nitroglycerin is given every five minutes under his tongue and blood pressure taken every five minutes before three doses are given. After fifteen minutes his blood pressure reads one hundred thirty over seventy and pulseoximeter reads ninety six percent on two liters of oxygen via nasal cannula. I ask him how he is feeling and he replies," The chest pain is completely gone and I feel much better, just extremely tired Doc." His ekg reading is normal at this time. I ask Nurse David to draw some blood work while I evaluate his current medications. He is allergic to aspirin so I will have to check his blood work before administering a blood thinner. I will have his blood work picked up within the hour and then will be able to substantiate between a single cardiac event or a possible heart attack. Inmate Brown has a history of hypertension and had a heart attack at the age of forty eight. He will be fifty five next week and is due for his annual physical in just a few days. It is time for me to go home as well as Nurse Marthagail. Nurse David Bentley will be working twelve hour night shift, 1500-0300 military time for three pm-three am. I give Nurse David orders to redraw his blood in six hours and to call me when his lab report is available from his initial lab work. Keep inmate Brown here in the infirmary overnight for observation and I will revaluate him in the morning after all of his blood work is is finished. Please call me with any problems or any questions you may have with this being your first solo night shift alone. He replies," I definitely will Doc. Everything will be fine." I was dreaming of being on a boat with my husband Michael when the phone rings and jolts me awake. " Inmate Sollie Brown began to experience chest pain with shortness of breath at 0200(two am) and I called an ambulance ten minutes ago," he said with a soft voice. I will be there in twenty minutes and thank you for calling. I arrive at 0230 and the paramedics are performing cpr (cardio pulmonary resuscitation). He is flat lined on the monitor as they shock him one last time. They arrived twenty minutes before I did. Will Drost and Rudy Harsan are very good paramedics whom I have known for many years. Rudy says," Hey Doc! Sorry we weren't able to revive inmate Brown." Will asks," Would you like me to call Dr. Sutton? I know you like to call him but I thought I would ask anyway." Thank you both for your hard work always but no thank you, I will call him. He likes to stop here and evaluate the patient and then he decides whether to transfer to the morgue or he signs the death certificate and has me transfer directly to the funeral parlor chosen by the inmate and or family. As the medics pack up their equipment, the both wave as they exit the infirmary. Nurse David bows his head and says," I feel so bad Doc! I initiated cpr right after I spoke to you and five minutes later he became unresponsive with no breath sounds. Five minutes into cpr, the paramedics arrived and took over." I am sure you did your very best, just make sure you chart everything. Dr. Sutton will need your report along with the complete medical record printed out before he arrives. He will need a transfer body to the county morgue or funeral parlor form which is in the filing cabinet under discharge/transfer tab. I will be in my office doing some paperwork if you need anything. Dr. Sutton arrives to my office and says," You have perfect timing my friend! I was just leaving the county morgue after performing two autopsies. A husband and wife, murder suicide. Have any of your famous coffee?" I can make you a fresh pot while you assess Inmate Sollie Brown. His medical record is on the table beside the gurney. As the coffee pot drips the last few drops ,

Dr. Sutton enters my office and says with his charming voice, “You can call the guards to transfer him to your morgue and I will draw some fluids to be analyzed then you can make arrangements to have his funeral parlor of choice pick him up.” Thank you for stopping in Jay. It is always a pleasure to see an old friend. “So while we drink some coffee, you can fill me in on your visitors. Have the agents made any headway yet?” he asked. They have all of our records as well as all of the open cases from the hospitals. Captain Jake turned over tapes from the morgue bay cameras which he said he was unable to make out the driver or the license plate of the black van but Nurse Claudia is visible handing a red cooler through the window. “No shit! Unbelievable that gorgeous creature is obviously a murderer and organ thief!” he said with a disgusted look upon his face and in the same breath adds,” I could get cozy with that goddess criminal!” You are so bad! We can’t refer to her as a murderess and organ thief until she is convicted but all the same, I believe you are right. “I would like to know how the hell she performs all of that work by her damn self! She has to have a partner!” he said with dismay. The FBI are calling all of her known family members and friends as well as the entire staff here for interviews. Her daughters and grand daughter have visited and are signed in on the visitor logs. Agent Alice Brubaker has an amazing track record as well as her partner Agent Donna Jean Bowke. I will keep you updated. Captain Jake informed me that Sgt. Ray Kirsh is being interviewed tomorrow morning. " Nurse Claudia Kirsh! Well no shit! He is her husband! I never put the names together before now! He is as handsome as she is beautiful, so I guess they make a nice looking couple. If I wasn't happily married, I would have asked her for a date." he said with an impish grin. You better behave yourself mister as we laugh together. We follow the guards to the morgue and I gather the supplies for Dr. Sutton to draw fluids from the eyes as well as the bladder. He proceeds to draw fluid from the liver and puts the fluids into separate specimen jars, labels them and puts them into bio hazard bags to drop off at his lab on his way home. "Well, you can make your arrangements and I will exit through the morgue bay employee entrance. You take care of yourself my friend and I will see you in class Tuesday." he said with a smile. I return to my office and Nurse David is straightening up the bay along with cleaning the gurney and applying fresh sheets. I grab my bag from my office and let him know that I am going home. I thank him as I exit the infirmary. He waves with a smile and says," Anytime Doc! I really like working here. Have a safe drive home." Nurse Marthagail will be clocking in soon, I think to myself on my drive home. She was coming in a few hours late today because she stayed two hours over training Nurse David. I am going to take a nap before my entirely long day today that will begin entirely too soon. I have to teach at the medical school this evening as well as sit in on a few interviews per Agent Donna Jean Bowke's request. She transferred from the unsolved homocide division before partnering up with Agent Alice Brubaker and the task force division. Agent Donna Jean is five foot eight, slender, with light brown hair and piercing blue eyes. She has a kind but stern voice and when she is deep in thought, her eyes look like blue icicles. Off to bed because eight A.M. is going to come entirely too soon. The alarm clock beeps and I just want to turn it off and go back to sleep. I swear! I should really take Michaels advice and retire so we can sail the ocean from continent to continent! Off to work I go! As I enter my office, my message light on my phone is lit up like a Christmas tree. Nurse Marthagail comes out of the medication room with empty boxes and enters my office and says" Good morning sunshine! How are ya doing darlin! You look so tired my dear and I don't mean to sound mean. I know you had a busy morning. Nurse David gave me a good report and had everything so neat and tidy when I got here. He is a keeper!" Good, I am glad you are happy with him because I am too so far. I have to sit in for a few interviews today with Agent Donna Jean, finish the monthly schedules and teach at the medical school this evening. I am going to have to drink five pots of coffee to make it through today my dear. “ You are so crazy! Have the agents gotten any further with their investigation?” she asked with her ever so charming southern accent. They have many interviews to conduct and hopefully their IT department will be able to get a more clear visual on the tapes Captain Jake turned over to Agent Alice Brubaker. “Captain Jake is very good at his job. I heard the cameras were down for a week and he wouldn’t stop following the IT guy until they were fixed. I just remembered something. The camera’s were down the week Nurse Claudia was here and she heard Captain Jake in the hallway as we were going to the cafeteria for breakfast the day I oriented her. ”she said with her eyebrows raised. Well! I will let Captain Jake know that little doozy of information! He will be happy to know that Nurse Claudia thought she wasn’t being taped at the morgue bay entrance and Agent Alice Brubaker is going to love this information because she is interviewing Sgt. Ray Kirsh today. Our very own loveable Lamar told Jake he was driving the transport bus around to the garage and saw him standing by the morgue entrance bay door alone one day.

CHAPTER 5

He stopped to ask him if he was expecting a delivery and he replied no that he was just taking a quiet break alone. “ The story just seems to be getting better and better for the agents investigation, ain’t it my pretty boss?” she said with a smile. It is beginning to look that way my dear. “Oh no! I hear that crazy boy John comin our way!” she laughs as she runs to the medication room. He begins raising his voice as he enters the infirmary, “Hey Doc. G! How ya doing? Have you raised enough hell back here yet?” You are not funny John! “I just stopped by to say hell to my favorite Doc G and to let you know that Guard Caroline and Guard Shelley are bringing down Inmate Benjamin Chad Russl in a wheelchair and hell yes I am too funny!” he says with a huge smile. Thank you John. I call out to him, you are not funny! as he waves and laughs out the infirmary door and holds it open for the guards arrival pushing the wheelchair. Inmate Ben has his head down and his left arm hanging down lower than his right as he is slouched towards his left as well. I will assist you both with him onto the gurney.

Nurse Marthagail exit's the medication room and assists also. I tell her to grab IV equipment and a heparin bag to hang. She brings out the blood test machine that checks how thin the blood is immediately along with the lab work trays. He has a history of several mini strokes. His face is drooped on the left side as I begin my assessment and Nurse Marthagail starts and IV, draws blood and checks his blood clotting time on the machine. His reading is within normal range to begin infusing the Heparin drip. His vital signs are normal but his physical assessment shows weakness upper and lower left extremities. I ask him how he is feeling and he responds with garbled speech," I am feeling pretty crappy Doc." I will get you to feeling better soon. If you don't improve within the hour I will have to transfer you to the hospital. An hour goes by and his facial droop is gone with his left upper arm improved strength as well as his left lower leg. How are you feeling now Ben? With clear speech and a soft voice replies," I feel better but very weak doc." Your vital signs are normal now as earlier. You get some rest and we will keep an eye on you for twenty four to forty eight hours and as long as you improve you can then return to your cell. If you worsen at anytime, I will have to send you to the hospital. " I understand doc. Thank you for taking good care of me." he said with a weak smile. Nurse Marthagail says," It is almost time for Nurse David to arrive which means I git to go home and argue with Lamar as she laughs." You and sweet Lamar fight like cats and dogs as I laugh. She replies," If you think he is so sweet, you take him home with you! We have been married over fifty years and I imagine the arguing is what keeps us together." We both laugh together as I tell her that she can keep him at her home and I will enjoy his laugh and visits here. Nurse David Bentley arrives for his shift as Nurse Marthagail gives him report before she leaves to meet Lamar and run errands on their way home. I finish reading emails and answering a few and then put together budget reports to deliver to Warden Andrew on my way out of the prison. As I pick up my bag and brief case to leave home to teach at the medical school my phone rings. " Sorry to bother you Doc, but Inmate Brown has taken a turn for the worse and is experiencing stroke symptoms. I called an ambulance and they are on their way." he said with a calm voice. I will be there in twenty minutes. As I enter the infirmary, the paramedics are standing beside the gurney. Inmate Sollie Brown is intubated and the heart monitor is reading a flat line. Paramedics Tabitha Bowke and Rachel Bowke have a saddened look upon their faces. Tabitha says," Hey Doc. I am sorry but we tried to revive him. He had a facial droop on the left side and his pupils were fixed and dilated bilaterally upon our arrival." Rachel adds," Would you like for me to call Dr. Sutton and get an order to transport him to the county morgue?" No thank you, I will call him. He comes here and assesses the decedent and will give me an order after he decides whether to transport the body to his county morgue or sign the death certificate and have him transported to his funeral parlor of choice. They pack up their equipment and both say," See ya Doc!" I have Nurse David enter his final notes into his charting and print out his medical record for Dr. Sutton. I proceed to my office to call Dr. Sutton and pull the necessary forms he will need when he arrives. He answers the phone after the first ring," Hello my friend! Are you on your way to the school?" Not hardly. Could you please stop by the infirmary. Inmate Brown expired within the last hour from stroke symptoms he began to experience yesterday. I was holding him for observation in which he had been stable until then. I will give you a more thorough report after you arrive. "On my way and thank you for the call as always." he replied with a kind voice. He arrives as I am sitting at my desk reviewing Inmate Brown's medical record. " Hello my friend! You look deep in thought." he says with a concerned voice. I am reviewing everything since Sollie Brown arrived yesterday and I don't understand how he declined so quickly after my last evaluation this afternoon.

His heparin IV was infusing and the intravenous site was patent then and the paramedics informed me that it was patent when they began working on him as well. “Let’s assess him together and we will figure this out Doc.” he said with compassion. As we finish his assessment together he says,” Have the guards transport him to the morgue and we will draw some fluids then I will have you make arrangements after his family see’s him to perform an autopsy in the morning here.” That sounds like a plan. We better head over to the medical school right now. We will make it just in time if traffic has eased up. I arrive to my office and the voicemail light is blinking on my office phone. I listen as Agent Alice Brubaker asks me to stop by the office anytime during my shift today for an update on Nurse Claudia. I look at the mail in my incoming file box and Dr. Sutton arrives with two large cups of coffee from our favorite place since college, The Donut Hole. He asks,” Are you ready to work with me my smart friend?” I am always obliged to work with you my oldest and dearest friend. Nurse Marthagail stops by the office as she puts supplies away and hands me a syringe she found under the gurney mattress that Inmate Brown occupied before he was transported to the morgue. She says,” Looky, looky what Nurse David missed when he stripped the sheets from the gurney. I always flip the mattress and sanitize both sides after an inmate occupies them." I show it to Dr. Sutton and he looks at it through the bio hazard bag. Thank you my thorough dear heart. Dr. Sutton adds," Thank you very much. I will send this to the forensics lab along with the specimens we collect from the autopsy this morning." We pull Inmate Brown from the cold storage unit and gather the supplies needed for his autopsy. As I pull the sheet off from his body, the intubation tube remained in place until Dr. Sutton removes it along with any other lines in place per standard protocol after any death in a medical facility. He says with sarcasm, " This is stellar! Somebody was very thoughtful in performing the autopsy for us!" I sit down to gather my composure for a minute before I scream with frustration. What in the hell is this shit! I honestly can't believe my eyes right now Jay! " I am here my friend and we will figure this out together as we always do. I am as angry as you are and I will do everything I can to bring justice to him and his family," he said with a stern voice. Before we begin, I have to call Warden Andrew and Captain Jake to review the tapes for the last twenty four hours from the infirmary and here in the morgue. As Dr. Sutton begins removing the sutures from the Y incision and opens the chest cavity, he says," The heart, lungs liver and kidneys are gone. Very professional job by someone with medical skills of great precision." That doesn't surprise me any longer Jay! I have another murderer and organ thief in our midst and I am going to wring their neck when I find out who it is! I have to met with Agent Alice Brubaker today and if you have time, you are welcome to accompany me Jay. "I will call my forensics lab courier and have these fluids picked up along with the syringe. I have to draw the vitreous humor from both eyes, then I will call the lab and accompany you to meet the girl scout," he says with an impish grin. As I put Inmate Brown back into cold storage and clean up, the courier arrives at the morgue entrance door to pick up all of the specimens and the syringe. Jay and I exit the morgue to the elevator to see Agent Alice Brubaker. I knock on the door of the office that the agents are occupying and Agent Alice Brubaker responds,

" Please come in." As Dr. Sutton and I enter the office, she has a welcoming smile and says," Hello Dr. Reaper! So nice to see you again and who may this handsome gentleman accompanying you be?" Dr Sutton extends his hand and introduces himself with his charming demeanor exposed," This handsome gentleman be, Dr. Jay Sutton, M.D.. I am Grayson County Coroner and I have a general practice locally as well. Nice to meet you Agent Brubaker." John is smirking in his chair located at the corner of the desk and says," Handsome gentleman not! I am the only handsome gentleman in this room!" Warden Andrew Joseph and Captain Jake give him the look of dismay that he is very used to receiving when he is being his usual comedic self at an inappropriate moment. John just rolls his eyes at them as usual. Agent Alice Brubaker says, " Yes you are John!" Everyone starts to laugh and she offers us to join them all by taking a seat. She says," Warden Andrew has updated me on yesterday's unexpected death and Captain Jake has brought the tape from the last twenty four hours to view together. I have the US Attorney's office issuing warrants to search Nurse Claudia's home and vehicles as we speak. Our IT department was not able to identify the driver or license plate of the black utility van on the tape we received but they were able to pull traffic camera footage in which we now have identified the driver as well as have the license plate number. The van has been located just ten miles from here and it has been traced back to the owner whom reported it stolen the very same evening it was seen on your tape. The driver is Ray Kirsh. We have enough evidence against both Claudia and Ray Kirsh to issue arrest warrants. We will pick them up when we issue the warrant to search their home and vehicles within the hour." That is great news Agent Brubaker! She replies, "Thank you Dr. Reaper. Let's view this tape and hopefully we will be able to view everybody that entered the infirmary and the morgue that were not authorized." The tape shows my nurses, the paramedics, Dr. Sutton, myself and the guards transporting Inmate Brown out of the infirmary. A cloth is placed over the camera for ten minutes and removed just a minute prior to the paramedics arrival per the date and time stamp on the tape. John blurted out with anger," I knew that crazy bitch had a partner! I knew there was no friggin way she could perform all of that work alone!" "Calm down little brother. We feel your anger and she will meet justice soon." Jake said as he placed his hand on John's shoulder. "Damn right we will! My role as Warden is going to make a monumental mark the day Nurse Claudia and Ray Kirsh and now their partner is placed behind bars. I am going to make a special request to have Ray Kirsh placed in a very cozy cell here when he is convicted!" Warden Andrew said with a stern angry voice. Dr. Sutton says," I will be happy to assist you all anyway I can." I can't wait to sit in court and watch them both go down! My inmates deserve justice and I will assist you as well! Agent Alice Brubaker says," We will all work together to find justice and I am happy to have you all working with me. If nobody else has anything to add this meeting, you all have been very helpful and thank you all for participating." As everyone leaves the office she asks me to stay for a few minutes. " Do you have an employee file for Nurse David

Bentley? I am going to call him in for an interview and I would like to review his employee history and check his nurse's license history as well." Yes. I have the records from the medical staff temp agency as well as a copy of his license and background check information in my office. "I will stop by your office after lunch to pick it up if you don't mind." she asked kindly. You can stop by my office anytime you like agent. We are on the same team to bring down everybody involved in killing my inmates, disgracing my infirmary and taking away precious loved family members from good family oriented people that I have met here. I took an oath to help the sick and care for these inmates, not to have them murdered right under my nose! "We will bring everyone involved to justice doc." she said with a serious expression on her face. As I exit the elevator and pass Captain Jake's office, I find the door locked and as I peek into his office window, the blind is open and his office is unoccupied. I then pass Guards Chad Bowke and Brandon Bowke to ask them if either of them know where He is currently located. Chad replies, Hey doc! He radioed his location about ten minutes ago from cell block D. John radioed for assistance on a medical call and Cap was closest to his vicinity." Brandon adds," What's up doc! Smiles and continues to say, Inmate Doug Rapkich is giving John hell as usual and during his usual threatening verbal abuse, began to pant and grasp his chest." Radio him now and ask them to bring him to the infirmary please. I am headed there now to set up the gurney with Nurse Marthagail. Thank you both and nice to see you both. They wave as Chad radios Captain Jake with my order. I decide to turn around and head to cell block D to look in on Inmate Rapkich while he is being placed in a wheelchair for transport to the infirmary. I arrive to the designated cell as John pushes him out of the cell and into the hallway. "Hey Doc G! What ya doing down here in the jungle? You came down to spy on us, didn't ya?" John quips with his Cheshire cat grin. I smile at him while Jake gives him a stink eye. I was on my way back to my office and while passing your office, I passed the guards and asked where you were located. I decided to meet up with you and check on Inmate Rapkich before he is brought to the infirmary. How are you feeling now Doug and when exactly did your symptoms begin? Through the facial grimacing and holding his chest he replies," Sgt. John made me sick and now I am having a heart attack doc! I feel good enough to give you a big and hard gift from my crotch though! You can be my grim reaper anytime!" As we continue walking together towards the infirmary, John pushing the wheelchair stops suddenly and faces Inmate Rapkich to say," You sick disrespectful bastard! I will beat you within an inch of your life and you will forget all about your fake chest pain! You are to respect her at all times or you will regret it!" "Then when John is done whipping your ass, I will make you wish you only had a complaint of chest pain! You feel me!" Jake voiced vehemently. "Okay, okay! Sorry doc." he said with an evil smile. Let's get to the infirmary at a quicker pace boy's please. We enter the infirmary and while Jake and John assist him to a standing position and seats him onto the gurney. Jake applies cuffs to his wrists and ankles then secures them with shackles to the gurney frame. Inmate Rapkich is currently serving a life sentence without parole. Convicted as the most notorious serial rapist and murderer in history. He stands at six feet two inches and weighs three hundred pounds of pure muscle. Shaves his head bald, blue eyes of pure ice and an evil smile that chills you to the bone. His skin is fair with skull tattoo's on seventy percent of his body. A black widow spider and black webs cover his entire scalp. As I perform my assessment and check vital signs, Nurse Marthagail approaches with the ekg machine and attaches the leads for an immediate reading. He has a history of hypertension but his vital signs and ekg are normal at this time. Jake and John stand on either side of the gurney and observe our work. Captain Jake waits for me to finish my assessment while Nurse Marthagail draws his blood, before saying," Inmate

Rapkich will have two guards posted on watch every shift. His shackles are not to be removed at anytime in which all of my guards are aware. None of the medical staff is to have direct contact with him unless the guards are standing directly next to him, and this includes you too doc!" Jake says with stern authority. Nurse Marthagail administered aspirin, nitroglycerin under his tongue once and his routine blood pressure medication before she drew his blood work. I ask him how he is feeling now and he replies," I feel much better doc, just tired." I tell Jake and John that he will be staying in the infirmary overnight for observation. They both nod their heads yes and as I thank them and walk back towards my office I overhear John tell him with a stern voice," Maggot! If you give any staff member a hard time, especially doc, your life sentence will become a death sentence very quickly!" Jake adds," I dare you to say one more inappropriate word or even look at her in any wrong way! You will beg to be placed in the electric chair by the time I am finished whipping your ass!" Rapkich replies, Oh give it a rest dynamic dick duo! I will be a true gentleman while I am here. I have nothing but respect for the doc man!" As I approach the bay, I tell him that he is going to be on his best behavior as well as respectful while he is being treated by my staff and myself. He nods his head yes and smiles at me with that evil look that sends chills up my spine. Jake informs me before I walk back to my office," I hired some new guards that start this afternoon and night shift. Tallon and Mathew Harsan will be here this afternoon and Guard Jim Williams will be training Claire Harsan and Stephanie Bowke on night shift." Good, I like Jim Williams. I always get a good laugh from his jokes. He is funnier than you John! "Hey Doc G! That's not even remotely true! You just don't get my twisted sense of humor is all! Right?" John said with a pout.

CHAPTER 6

You know you are my favorite twisted comedian John! Jake says with sarcasm," Hey! You told me I was your favorite guard of all time!" You both are my favorite guards so deal with it! I smile at them and return to my office to put a medical file together while Inmate Rapkich is here. I add notes to his record on the computer before printing it out. My phone rings and I answer it before it rings twice. "Hello my friend! How are you today?" asks Dr. Sutton. Hello to you my old friend! I am fine today and you? " I am well and thanks for asking. I received reports from the forensics lab and you are not going to believe it! The fingerprints on the syringe that was found under the gurney mattress where Inmate Brown was laying on, belongs to Nurse Marthagail and Nurse Claudia Kirsh! There was also a third fingerprint on the syringe that hasn't been identified yet. The fluid analyzed in the syringe was tetrodotoxin." Oh my God! I can't even begin to respond to that! Nurse David Bentley was on duty when Inmate Brown expired but she was on duty that day until 3 P.M.! There is no way I am going to remotely believe she has any wrong doing with his death! There has to be a valid explanation for her fingerprints being present on that syringe! " The lab work we collected also has tetrodotoxin present doc. I am sorry to have upset you my friend but I am just relaying all of the results to you. I forwarded my findings to Agent Alice Brubaker right before I called you." he said with a kind voice. Well I am certain she will get to the bottom of this and exclude her from any of this mess! "I hope you are right doc! You always had a good intuition when it comes to good and bad feelings towards people. I honestly hope you are right this time too." he said with an assuring voice. You are the leading forensics pathology physician on these cases, so have you heard anything further upon the whereabouts of Nurse Claudia and her husband Ray yet? "I just came from an early morning meeting before I arrived to see you and the FBI has had nothing as of now. They teamed up with the US Marshall Service for assistance as well." he replied with a slight arrogance . That's great! I overheard her speaking to Nurse Marthagail during new employment orientation regarding relatives she had just visited in Toronto, Canada and how she would love to live there after she retires. He stands up and says," Hell! Maybe that's where she is hiding now! I will call Agent Alice Brubaker and inform her immediately!" My phone rings and as I pick up the receiver, Captain Jake replies," Hey Doc! Warden Andrew just called me and wanted me to gather everyone for a last minute meeting scheduled in one hour requested by Agent Brubaker." Thank you so much for letting me know Captain. As I place the receiver back in the cradle, Dr. Sutton raises his brows. That was Captain Jake notifying me of a last minute meeting being held in an hour with Agent Brubaker. Would you like to accompany me and tell her the information in person? " I sure would Doc. I happen to have the rest of the day open." he said with a smile. Maybe she has an update on their present location and are apprehending them as we speak. That would be great news! Dr. Suttons cell phone rings and he answers," Dr. Sutton here. His forehead wrinkles up as he listens as he says thank you for the update Officer Droste." He then comments," The Grayson County Sheriff's Department is pulling prints on every staff member here to compare with the third print on the syringe and will let me know as soon as they get a hit with AFIS as well as the NCIC data base as well." Wow! This is the most information we have heard in two weeks! Let's hope Agent Alice Brubaker has the icing on the cake information for us today.

As Dr. Sutton and I walk out of my office, Nurse Marthagail approaches us. She says," I received a call in my office from reception and Nurse David Bentley will not be reporting for duty today. The Agency is sending another nurse to cover him." Thank you for letting me know my friend. I am going to a meeting with the warden right now and when I get back I will call the Agency and find out who they are sending over so Captain Jake can meet them at the front entrance to sign them in and issue a temporary staff badge for the shift. All agency staff is issued a temporary badge each shift they work because they are employed with an outside agency that this facility is contracted with. There are only two temp agencies we use here to cover staff in this entire facility. I will ask Captain Jake if the Grayson Sheriffs Department pulled the temp agencies employee fingerprints to run along with our prison staff as well. "Well Doc! You are a smart cookie! I would not have thought about the outside agency staff that fills in here myself! You can ask Captain Jake that amazing question when we see him in a few minutes." he said with that famous Cheshire Cat grin. As we enter the conference room, every seat is filled and Warden Andrew is standing beside Agent Brubaker at the podium. I close the door and Warden Andrew asks us all to have a seat so we can begin. "Welcome all and thank you for attending this last minute important meeting. Agent Alice Brubaker is going to lead this meeting," he said with a stern look and deep voice. "Hello to all of you and thank you for attending. The FBI is working very diligently alongside the US Marshall Service to locate Claudia and Ray Kirsh but have not made any progress at this time. We have had no tips from the tip lines we set up ." she said with an annoyed voice. As she begins to continue speaking, Dr. Sutton raises his hand and asks," Have you looked into other countries for them? The reason I ask is because Doc and I were speaking in her office, she remembered overhearing Nurse Claudia speaking with Nurse Marthagail on her first day that she had just visited relatives in Toronto, Canada and would like to live there when she retires." I raise my hand and ask if the employees we utilize from temp agencies had their fingerprints run along with our regular staffs. Captain Jake gives me a look with raised eyebrows and a thumbs up. Agent Brubaker replies," To answer your amazing questions is a pleasure. As she opens the file in front of her, she continues to say, I see no notations on Canada but we have spoken with Interpol to assist us as well. I will call the Grayson field office and have them send out the teams immediately. The temp agencies that are contracted here was visited by our forensics team for files and fingerprints this morning and thanks to Captain Jake's phone call to me this morning my office was able to get a warrant in a very timely manner. Each and every staff member here has been an amazing asset to me and my team. I came here to update you all on what we had not achieved thus far and with your information I am very hopeful that we will be able to finally bring Claudia and Ray Kirsh to justice and their accomplice very soon,' she said with a smile and claps her hands. Warden Andrew says," If there is no questions or further comments, I would like to end this meeting with a positive note. I am privileged to work with each and every one of you. The team work and constant dedication you all give on the job makes me very proud. With your exemplary work, Agent Brubaker is exactly right with the possible and very soon apprehension we all are ready for as he claps his hands along with Agent Brubaker one last time." We all stand up and join in on the clapping.

Another day begins with the monthly budgets due and just when I finish with the staffing schedule, a voice from the entrance doorway bellows," Hey Doc Grim! How the hell are you?", John laughs as he speaks. Where have you been John? It has been very quiet this past week. I smile at him as I stand up to welcome him into my office and point at the chair as he sits down with a thud. He replies with a crooked smile," I was on vacation all week Doc and I know damn well that you missed this handsome face along with my amazing humor!" Yeah I sure did young man. I don't know how I survived this entire week without you! I am laughing along with him as he lowers his head imitating that his feelings are hurt. He then lifts his head and says," I know you missed me Doc! Nobody can make you laugh like me!" Did you go anywhere in particular on your vacation? " I rode my Soft tail Harley to West Virginia and bungee jumped from the New River Gorge Bridge with my best friend Hunter. He rode his Fat Boy Harley and we camped by the river for a few days then traveled to Pennsylvania and camped at Cooks Forest. We took a three mile canoe ride before traveling back home ." That sounds like an amazing adrenaline rush bungee cord jumping. I knew you were crazy John, but not that crazy! "I have always wanted to see the New River Gorge but Hunter talked me into jumping. It didn't take much coaxing though, so yeah, I am that crazy Doc!' he laughs as he tells his story. Well John, I am glad you made it back safely. My extension rings as we are talking and I answer. Hello Captain Jake! How are you? He answers," I am fine Doc. I am calling to inform you of a meeting scheduled for Friday morning at ten. Agent Alice Brubaker has some important news to update us with." John says," Hey Captain America!" Jake replies," Oh no! He is back from vacation already! He is on the schedule for tomorrow as I look at it now as he is laughing the entire time of his response." John replies," Yeah, yeah! I know you missed the greatest guard here!" The phone was put on speaker after I answered it as Jake replies," I can't miss myself Johnny boy!" Ok children! Thank you for letting me know Jake. I will see you Friday but surely before then also. I am going to chase John out of my office so I can finish my staff schedules. He laughs as he hangs up the phone. "Ok, ok I will let you get back to your fun work Doc! I will see you tomorrow when I report for duty. Have a good day Doc Grim!" he says while laughing as he exit's the infirmary. Nurse Marthagail enters my office with a smile and says," I see Mr. Crazy is back! It was awful quiet while he was away. I will never tell him to his face, but he is very funny and he could make a dog laugh. His head would grow too big to fit through the doorway if I told him." I agree with you. He is a good man and he jokes around with everybody in which we all need in this sad environment sometimes. Captain Jake called to let me know about a meeting Friday morning with Agent Brubaker. “Well! That sounds promising considering she was just here Friday. I hope she has good news finally,” she said sternly. I sure hope she does as well my friend. The medical staffing agency called and they are sending Nurse Grace Lowe the rest of the week. I asked about Nurse David Bentley and they said he quit without a notice. She replied,” I wonder why he quit so suddenly. I hope Agent Brubaker got in touch with him. She questioned me a few weeks ago and asked me if I had heard from him since he left. I told her no and I only spoke to him during change of shift report and no other time.” I will ask her Friday whcn I see her before the meeting. She stops by my office for coffee before the meetings and the one day a week she uses the office upstairs.

As I sit at my desk working on quarterly budget reports a knock on my office door welcomes Agent Alice Brubaker. Good morning Agent Brubaker! Please come in and have a seat. She smiles as she sits down and says," Good morning Doc! I have some updates that I wanted to give directly to you before the meeting scheduled for tomorrow afternoon. Warden Joseph and Chrissy are notifying all of the staff currently so I decided to pay you a visit myself." I am always happy to see you my friend. Please tell me you have some good news. "My forensics lab finished evaluating all of the syringes and insulin bottles in all of the sharps containers obtained from the infirmary and the morgue. Five syringes contained Tetrodotoxin and one syringe contained Tetrodotoxin and Promethazine which also had Nurse Martha Gails fingerprints as well as Nurse David Bentleys. The five other syringes had Nurse Claudias fingerprints and Nurse David Bentleys as well as an unidentified fingerprint that has been processing through all of our databases for several days with no hits yet. I questioned Nurse Martha Gail and after evaluating all of her medical charting along with Nurse David Bentleys, she opend a syringe and drew up Promethazine to administer intramuscularly to Inmate Brown and handed it to Nurse David Bentley to discard into the sharps container. That was the syringe that also contained Tetrodotoxin and had his fingerprints on as well. All of the syringes and bottles had her fingerprints on them and matched her medication documentation as well. One of the insulin bottles had fast acting insulin present as well as Tetrodotoxin residue. Nurse David Bentley and Nurse Claudia's fingerprints were on that multiuse fast acting insulin vial and only that vial. Another multiuse fast acting insulin vial was explained in your medication documentation as well as Nurse Martha Gail's, Nurse Claudia's, Nurse David Bentley's and your fingerprints were present on this vial also. Nusre Martha Gail was cleared from this investigation," she said with smile that warmed my heart. That is great news! Thank you so much for taking the time to visit and taking the burden off my worrisome heart Agent Brubaker. I knew Nurse Martha Gail couldn't have committed murder. She is a genuinely good person with a compassionate soul that beams goodness everywhere she goes. I have had faith in your ability to catch the guilty ever since I met you and I am sure you will bring all guilty parties to justice soon. "I thank you for your faith in me Doc. My team and I will bring everyone involved to justice together. The help we receive from you and your team has brought us closer to catching Nurse Claudia along with her accomplices. We have the evidence we need to prosecute our case now, we just have to locate Claudia and Ray Kirsh as well as David Bentley so we can pick them up and prosecute them to the fullest extent of the law," she said vehemently. That will be a great day to

celebrtare and bring closure to the families they brought so much sadness to. I will definitely be present in court to witness justice for all of the families she took so much from. "I have to return to my office Doc. I will see you tomorrow afternnon at the meeting," she said as she stands up to exit the office. Thank you for stopping by my office agent. Her cell phone rings as she exits the infirmary door. John opens the infirmary door as Agent Brubaker exits and she thanks him for holding the door open for her as he calls out," Hey Doc! How the hell are you this morning?" I hold my breath for a second as I think to myself, oh no! Hell on wheels is about to enter my office! Smiling and giggling as I brace myself for his visit, he enters my office and throws himself into the chair in front of my desk. How are you doing John? He replies with a crooked grin," I am just fine Doc! I was just notified by Captain Jake that we have a staff meeting tomorrow afternoon. Agent Brubaker just left your office, is
everything ok?" Yes John. She has visited frequently since her investigation began here. We have coffee the few days a week she has been occupying the office upstairs actually. She stops by before she leaves the facility to say hello which we both have become accustomed to. How have you been? "I wanted to say hello and just check in on you Doc," he said with a kind smile. "Comeon

Doc! I know you missed this handsome face!' he said as he laughs. Yes John. I always miss you and your crazy handsome face. I smile at him as he furrows hia eyebrows at my response. " I just wanted to stop by and check on you Doc!" he said with a serious voice. Thank you for stopping by John. I appreciate your concern. He stands up to exit my office and waves as he exit's the infirmary. My office phone rings as I close the office door and return to my desk. I push the intercom button and answer hello. "Hey Doc! How are you? Just wanted to let you know about the staff meeting scheduled for tomorrow afternnon at two." Warden Andrew Joseph said. Thank you for letting me know warden. Agent Brubaker just left my office and she let me know about the meeting. How have you been warden? " Same old crap different day Doc! How have you been? I wanted to let you know about the meeting and check on you myself," he said with a chuckle. I am always happy to hear from you warden! John just left my office and said the same thing as I laugh outloud. "You are well liked Doc! I will let you get back to work and I will see you tomorrow," he said as he laughs. I finally click the computer back on to finish budget reports then I have to finish the monthly staffing schedules. I am looking forward to the staff meeting tomorrow afternoon. Hopefully Agent Brubaker and her team will close this case very soon. I know everybody is anxious to get some good news and bring some justice to the many families of the inmates they wronged. Finishing last minute tasks before going home with another day closer to retirement. As I turn off the desk lamp the phone rings. I answer to Captain Jake on the line. “Hello Doc! I am glad I caught you before you left. Just wanted to let you know about the staff meeting tomorrow afternoon at two and just wanted to say hello and check on you,” he said ever so kindly. I feel so important today! Warden Joseph and John checked in on me as well as you! Agent Brubaker stopped by this morming and let me know about the staff meeting tomorrow afternoon though she and I meet for coffee a few days a week when she occupies the office upstairs. Thank you for checking up on me Jake! I really appreciate the attention I have gotten from you all today! “Anytime Ma’am! I will see you at the meeting tomorrow. Be safe going home,” he said as he hung up.

Another morning arriving to my office anticipating the outcome of the meeting this afternoon. I have the quarterly budget reports to drop off in the wardens office when I attend the meeting today. I will make copies of the staff schedule to hand out this morning and a copy for the main office. Nurse Martha Gail is putting supplies away so I will tidy up my office and the infirmary to pass time until the meeting. Checking all of the expiration dates on

the supplies and medications passed more time than I expected. It is noon already so I will ask Nurse Martha Gail if she wants to join me for lunch in the cafeteria, then I will assist her with the last of the supplies before attending the meeting.
“Thank you for all of your help Doc! I will break down these boxes and you better scoot to the meeting”, she said with her charming southern drawl.

CHAPTER 7

As I enter the conference room, everyone is standing at the table chatting amongst themselves. Warden Andrew Joseph walks in with Agent Alice Brubaker. They stand at the podium as warden welcomes everyone and asks us all to sit down. “Welcome all to this important meeting and I am going to turn the meeting over to Agent Alice Brubaker,” he said with a stern voice. “Hello everyone and thank you for being here. As of midnight, Canadian Mounties, US Marshalls and the FBI as a team effort picked up Claudia and Ray Kirsh in Toronto, Canada. David Bentley was at the same residence as we found out that not only was he their partner, but also a distant cousin of

Claudia's. We have compiled all of the evidence we need to prosecute them to the fullest extent of the law. They are all being held without bail with the US Marshalls until their trial dates are set," she said with a steady stern voice and smile. Warden Andrew Joseph says," Lets thank Agent Alice Brubaker and her team with the FBI for their professionalism and assistance closing this investigation and with our team work we all deserve a hand!" Everyone stands up and claps simultaneously.

CHAPTER 8

I finish up the few tasks in my office before going home and as I pick up my bags to leave my office, the phone rings. I answer on the second ring as Warden Andrew Joseph replies," Hey Doc! I just received an unexpected call from Agent Alice Brubaker. She is requesting an early morning meeting to update everyone on some new information that needs passed on immediately. Seven a.m. in the conference room. I notified all staff that needs to be present." Thank you for letting me know warden. I will be there with bells on. I tell Nurse Marthagail to have a nice evening and inform her that a new nurse was hired today and will arrive at three a.m. to relieve her. She worked here several years ago and after her maternity leave was up, she decided to take an extended leave of absence to raise her daughter. She replies with a smile," It's about dang time we get some help! That is great news Doc! Be careful on your travel home. What is that new nurses name anyhow?" Oh! I am so sorry my friend! My mind is on that early morning meeting and what it could entail. Her name is Bethany Rutt. Her name was Bethany Delick when she worked here three years ago. She got married and when she left on maternity leave she just extended it to raise her daughter. "I remember her very fondly! Yeah, yeah she was very meticulous with everything she did and always very professional and courteous." she replied with enthusiasm. See you tomorrow afternoon. I arrive home to Michael cooking on the grill along with John and Jake. John jumps out of his chair and sets his beer on the table as he approaches me with his arms wide open. He hugs me and says," Hey Doc Mama! How the hell are ya? Bet you are excited to see me!" Jake and Michael roll their eyes. Jake replies," Really John! You know I am Mama's favorite son!" Michael replies," You both are making me sick! I am her favorite of all!" A big shadow walks through the garage to the patio and replies," Whoa! I am Mamas favorite out of all of you clowns! I am the warden and what I say goes!" John quips," Not on these grounds ya ain't brother! Maybe in your castle you are but not here! Jake chimes in," Let's take it out into the yard and I will show you all whose boss here! And! The one and only favorite son always kicks your asses!" Oh boy's! Your Mama will kick all of your asses if you don't settle down. We all laugh. Let me get changed so we can sit down to these amazing steaks and beer and discuss what our morning meeting could possibly be about. We all sit at the patio table and brain storm. I ask Andrew what he thinks as he replies," I really don't know Mama. I heard about a US Marshall caravan was ambushed this morning while transporting two prisoners to the US District Courthouse in Grayson County." Oh my God! Wasn't Claudia and Ray Kirsh being transported to court this morning? I remember watching the news yesterday and the FBI Director announced their court date was approaching and he would give another news update after they were placed in jail awaiting arraignment. Jake replies," That has to be the caravan that was ambushed. I remember Ray telling me his brother was a US Marshall. I would love to get my hands around Ray's neck right about now!" John replies," Oh hell yeah! Let's go after him and Claudia!" Listen you all! We will all go to the meeting in the morning and just listen to what Agent Brubaker is going to tell us. If this is the case, then that is very sad! We all clean up and say

our goodbyes. To the shower and to bed for another day arrives tomorrow. I arrive to the infirmary to have Nurse Bethany greet me. "Good morning Doc! Been a few years huh. My daughter Emilee just turned a year old and my son Hayden is five years old already." she said with a beaming smile. Bethany is fair skinned with dark brown hair and brown velvet eyes that mesmerize you.
She stands five feet five and has a slender build. Honestly she looks as if she has never had a child. I could be jealous but I have always admired a woman that retains her body after carrying a child for nine months. How was your night Nurse Bethany? "IT was pretty uneventful besides one inmate complaining of a headache and his blood pressure was elevated enough to administer an as needed blood pressure medication. I rechecked his blood pressure thirty minutes after administration and it came down to normal with his headache subsiding completely." she said with a stern soft voice. Let me guess. It was Inmate Chuck Haywood. She replies," Yes it was certainly him. She laughs as she continues to say, you always were very good at knowing each and every inmates medical history Doc!" Yes. I have a photographic memory which came in very handy in medical school. I am going to a meeting in a few minutes. Do you need anything before I go upstairs? "No Doc. I even put some supplies away during the

night before Inmate Haywood with Guards Jimmy Williamson and his wife Robin. They are as funny as I remember," she said as she laughs. I have to agree with you. I have known them since high school and they have not changed a bit. I will return soon and if you want to catch up the past few years and I am sure you have some photos of those beautiful kids of yours. I arrive to the conference room with everyone talking amongst themselves. Warden Andrew and Agent Alice Brubaker are standing at the podium with very serious looks upon their faces. Warden Andrew Joseph puts his hand up and says," Agent Alice Brubaker has requested this meeting to update us upon the current situation regarding Claudia and Ray Kirsh." "Good morning and thank you all for attending this last minute meeting. The US Marshall caravan that was transporting Claudia and Ray Kirsh was ambushed on the way to Grayson County jail where they were to be held for arraignment Monday morning. Today being Friday and the ambush was yesterday morning. They have escaped in a newer black full sized SUV. No license plates and tinted windows so the driver was not visible on the closed circuit street cameras. We have all of their known families and associates being monitored closely but have had no success at this time. Traffic cameras lost the SUV in a parking garage and ten minutes after they entered SWAT entered the parking garage without success. The SUV was burning in the lowest level of the garage and though it has been towed to our garage for a full forensics review, I am doubtful anything will be found." she said with a look of disgust on her face. Captain Jake stands up and says," Agent Brubaker, Are you aware that Ray Kirsh has a brother that works for the US Marshall Service? His first name is Brian but his last name is different because they are stepbrothers. I remember Ray talking about him when he first started working here ten years ago." She replies with a smile," Well, well! Thank you so much for that information captain! That will definitely give us a head start in apprehending them all, starting with Mister Brian!" Captain Jake then replies," Happy to assist anyway I can agent. I will look into his employee records and update you with possibly naming his stepbrother Brian as an emergency contact." "That will be great! Thanks again Captain Jake!" she replied with enthusiasm. Warden Andrew Joseph says," Thank you Agent Brubaker for stopping in with that concerning update. If there is no other concerns or additions from anyone, that will end this meeting." We all begin to leave the conference room one by one when Agent Brubaker follows me out and asks if she can accompany me back to my office. We enter my office and she closes the door behind her. I offer her some coffee as she sits down in front of my desk and says," How are you Doc? Have you given any further thought about the career move I offered you?" No I haven't agent. I have been busy trying to keep my infirmary staffed since we last spoke. I just hired a nurse that worked here a few years ago and I am so pleased she is back. Nurse Marthagail is very happy to have her back as well. I will give some thought to that amazing opportunity soon and I will let you know. I have been doing well. Thank you for asking. How about you?" I was offered a promotion to lead up the Grayson field office with my own team. I will be over the Homocide Division with the ten years experience I had in Ohio as a homocide detective before deciding to attend Quantico and use my Psychology degree to become an FBI Agent. I had attended Ohio State University and graduated top of my class with my Doctorate in Psychology, then I decided to stay in college for Criminal Justice to become a police officer which just felt right for me. I was approached by an FBI agent during a high profile murder case that recommended that I put my degree to work for them as a profiler. We closed the case and I enrolled to Quantico that fall and have never regretted one minute of that decision." she said with that heart melting smile. That is wonderful! I was a registered nurse before deciding to attend medical school and now I teach one day a week at the medical school after working at the University of Kentucky Hospital as a doctor as well as teach full time. As my sons got older and I was looking into retirement options, I decided to work here and make a difference with the inmates. Since you offered me a new career opportunity would I be working with you when you transfer? She replies," Yes you will be working with me directly. You will be my partner if that's what you want." That sounds very interesting. I have ten years before I can retire and that career move would certainly be an exciting change. I will definitely give your offer some serious thought Agent Brubaker. "Please call me Alice Doc." she said with a smile. Ok Alice. Please call me Betty. We both laugh. "Thank you for the coffee Betty. I have to get back to my office and find out if there has been any updates on Claudia and Ray Kirsh. I have to stop to see Captain Jake on my way out and request a copy of Ray's employee file and maybe he has some information regarding his stepbrother Brian." she said with a serious voice. So nice to see you Alice and I will let you know when I decide to change my career path. She leaves the infirmary as John walks in. "Hey! What's up Doc! Can you believe that meeting? That is some bullshit with that escape!" he said with that Cheshire cat grin and his arms crossed. I agree with you entirely. "I just wanted to stop by and say hello and to let you know that Michael and I are planning a boating trip to Sandusky, Ohio. Lake Erie has some great fishing charters." he said with bright eyes resembling a child's on Christmas morning. Good! That means I will get a break from you both for a while. He furrows his brows and paces his right hand over his heart as I laugh. You can't have a broken heart John because you have to have a heart first. He replies," I have a great big heart Doc! You really know how to stab my heart for sure." We both laugh as he walks out of my office clutching his chest and laughing. I sit down at my desk to look at Inmate Haywood's medical chart to make sure Nurse Bethany didn't miss anything. Nurse Marthagail enters my office and says," I came in a few hours early to check in on Nurse Bethany and we straightened up the infirmary as well as organized the medicine cabinets. I am so glad she is back. Her youngens are absolutely adorable. I heard Claudia and Ray escaped custody on the news yesterday evening. Is that why Agent Brubaker was here today?" Yes it is my friend. I am as shocked as you are. Are you ok with me leaving in a few minutes? I have to stop at the university to meet with Dr. Jay Sutton. We revised the lab rotations for the medical school students and I have been promising to meet him for coffee for quite a while. "Sure Doc! If there is anything you need to know I will let you know directly. Go and have some fun." she said with that darling southern drawl. I wave at Nurse Bethany as I leave the infirmary and call out to her and say, I will catch up with you tomorrow morning when I arrive. She smiles and waves back.

CHAPTER 9

I arrive home finally after fighting traffic for almost an hour. I have the house all to myself for a week while Michael is on a trip to Virginia visiting old Navy buddies. After the USS Kansas City was decommissioned, they vowed to get together once a year. I will get a shower and relax by the fireplace with a good book and try not to think about Claudia and Ray's current whereabouts. My new book by Nora Roberts is the perfect distraction I need right now. As I turn the page to begin chapter three and reach for my glass of Merlot, my phone rings. I answer to Nurse Bethany's sweet voice," Hello Doc! I am sorry to bother you but you require a call when an inmate comes into the infirmary. Inmate Amos Moses was brought in fifteen minutes ago complaining of chest pain. I initiated the chest pain protocol orders and after the third dose of nitroglycerin sublingual his chest pain completely subsided. His initial blood pressure was one hundred sixty over ninety. The EKG was within normal limits. I printed it out and placed it in his chart for you to evaluate when you arrive in the morning. I will keep him here for observation for twelve hours per your protocol. If there is any further problems I will notify you immediately." Thank you so much for calling Bethany. You can always call me anytime and it is never a bother to get an update regarding my inmates. You have a good night and I will see you in the morning. "Thank you Doc. You do the same," she said. I am so glad Nurse Bethany returned to work for me. She is a very competent and compassionate nurse. Back to my exciting story of witches and the imagination of travel to Ireland. Just when I turn page after page to absorb her amazing descriptions of majestic beauty and intrigue my eyes get heavier and I just have to insert my butterfly bookmark and get to bed for some much needed sleep. Awakened by a ringing phone and not the familiar sound of my alarm. Grabbing my phone to see four A.M. and the caller ID reading Infirmary, I answer to Nurse Bethany's slightly distressed voice," Umm, morning Doc. As I evaluated Inmate Amos Moses, he was not breathing nor had a pulse. I called a code and an ambulance. The guards and I performed CPR until the medics arrived and they are here now." I will be there in twenty minutes. I arrive to the infirmary as the medics and Nurse Bethany are standing at the cart beside Inmate

Moses. Medics Andy and Ron shake their heads as I walk towards them. Andy says, “ Hey Doc. We performed CPR for twenty minutes without success. He was unresponsive and had no pulse when we took over. We shocked him three times and administered Epinephrine. Do you want me to call Dr. Jay Sutton?” No thanks. I will call him in. Our new protocol set by the warden is Dr. Sutton is to be called in for any inmates death before the body can be released. I have to call the family in as well. Just leave me a copy of your report for Dr. Sutton please. Thank you both for everything. “That’s what we do Doc!’, said Ron. They both wave as they exit the infirmary. Nurse Bethany says,” I will pick up the mess on the floor and finish my charting before Dr. Sutton arrives.” Just leave the mess for now. I will pick it up after Dr. Sutton and I evaluate Inmate Moses. Please print out your charting and place it in the chart with the medics report Bethany. Thank you for being here. You can give me a verbal report while we wait for Jay to arrive. “Sure Doc! I checked on Inmate Amos Moses every two hours. His vital signs were within normal limits since six P.M. No complaints of chest pain. He requested a snack at nine P.M. and rested comfortably. I checked on him at three forty five A.M. and that’s when he was unresponsive and had no pulse. I immediately called a code, called the ambulance and then you.”

she said with a stern voice. He had a history of hypertension but had been under control for the last year. Jimmy and Robin were on duty at six P.M. and will be here until six A.M. right? "Yes.", she replied. I will call them and ask what Inmate Moses was doing before they brought him to the infirmary. I place a call to the guards office to have dispatch radio guards Jimmy and Robin and ask them to stop by my office as soon as they can. I would like to have that information regarding Inmate Amos Moses's condition when they brought him to the infirmary to pass on to Dr. Jay Sutton when he arrives. Nurse Marthagail enters my office to ask," Hey there Doc. Is there anything I can do for you?" No thank you my friend. I pulled the forms out of the filing cabinet and put a chart together for Dr. Sutton already. How have you been? How is that handsome and charming Lamar doing? He hasn't stopped by the infirmary to see me for about a month. I always enjoy his stories from his childhood. His first job as an ambulance driver and a deputy sheriff for the small town he grew up in. I remember him telling me that the population was only 1,500 then. "Thanks for asking Doc! I have been busy with recognition dinners for the Masonic Lodge and Lamar was on vacation for three weeks. He only took one week vacation last year so he was mandated to use it this year. He has been spending a lot of time at the Masonic lodge for meetings and initiating new members that were signed in by relatives that have been thirty year members. Lamar just received his forty year pin. He is cantankerous as ever. If he is not driving me crazy, he has to find trouble to get into", she said with her charming southern drawl while laughing. That is very good to hear! She stands up to leave my office and says," It was so nice to have this brief chat Doc! I miss our lunch dates and casual conversations. Have you heard anything new regarding Claudia and Ray?" Not a thing as of yet. "I am going to straighten up the medication room and put away some stock. If you need anything you know where to find me," she says with a smile and waves as she exits my office. I hear the infirmary door beep from the badge swipe entry pad and Dr. Jay Sutton enters my office with a smile and two large coffees from our local diner and says," Good morning my beautiful friend! So sad that I only see you a few days a month in the lab at the medical school and when you have a death here. We need to get together for lunch or dinner and catch up. We always enjoy reminiscing about our glory days in college and especially medical school." Well Jay, you are always welcome to have dinner at my house. Mike has been cooking on the grill almost everyday. It gets really fun when my sons stop over and they would love to see you. Are you busy Friday? He replies," I am actually free on Friday. I scheduled an office day to work on my quarterly budgets but I have been working on them a little everyday the last week just so I could put aside the entire day away from the office. You have perfect timing my friend! I will bring wine for you and beer for us guys. I am really looking forward to Friday Doc! Let's take a look at Inmate Moses then we can finish chatting." I am actually leaving at lunch time today. Do you want to have lunch with me? We can go over the rotation schedule for the lab to hand out tomorrow. "Sure can my friend. Lets get this done and I will go to the office to work on assignments for the lab and we sync the rotation schedule and the assignments together." he said with that charming crooked smile he is well known for. He looks at the folder I handed him then places it by his bag on the bedside table. He opens his medical bag to take out syringes and tubes to draw blood along with his stethoscope. Listens to Inmate Moses chest then performs a precursory examination of the anterior and posterior body. Draws blood and extracts urine from the bladder with a syringe then places the urine sample into a specimen jar. Placing identification stickers from the chart onto the tubes and specimen container, he then places them into individual biohazard bags and seals them securely for transport in the travel laboratory specimen cooler. " I will deliver these specimens to the lab as

I head to my office. You can notify Stratton and Baroski to pick him up after his family arrives. I will walk to the office with you and finish my notes in this chart so you can make me a copy for my records. I am signing the death certificate and cause of death is Cardiac Arrest." he said with a stern voice. As soon as we sit down at my desk, I call the guards to transport Inmate Amos Moses to the morgue. His nieces will be here in an hour to pick up his personal belongings. As Jay finishes his notes, the infirmary door entry pad beeps with Jimmy and Robin walks through the door. "Hey Doc G! Laughing as he said it and Robin scowling at him. I know that is Johns line but I just had to say it anyhow! Sorry Doc. Sorry it took us a while to get down here." Jimmy said with a big grin on his face. " While rounding, we had to move a cellmate to an empty cell. Inmates Jack Henry and Philip Lane were fist fighting for the third time in the last three days. When you return to the unit, please send both of them down for evaluations. "Sure will Doc. During rounds yesterday, I passed Inmate Amos Moses cell and he was sleeping with a snore that would wake the dead. I left my clipboard on cellblock B so after I rounded cellblock C, I headed back towards B and as I passed Inmate Moses cell and he was sitting at the edge of his cot with his hand over his chest. I asked him if he was feeling alright and he said his chest hurting. I paged Jimmy and asked him to bring a wheelchair down immediately to cellblock C # 747. He looked pale and spoke with a soft voice." Robin said. Thank you for the information Robin. Jimmy, You don't have to be sorry because it was amusing that you borrowed Johns famous line for me! God knows that boy is hilarious but if we tell him that, his head won't fit through the doorway. We all laugh. Dr. Sutton stands up and hands me the file to make copies for him. Jimmy says," hello Doc Sutton! How the heck have you been? You are a very busy man! Exactly how many gang members got hit last week?" Dr. Sutton replies," Well Jim, four came to the morgue and three to Grayson Generals emergency room. Two of them transferred to ICU and the third young girl was brought to the morgue. The oldest gang member being just nineteen and the other five members were thirteen, fourteen and the other three just seventeen years old. I am so damn angry with these local gangs being run by children. I know their demographics are mostly single parent homes, foster kids that I am sure the parents didn't even report their absence and runaways that migrated into the gangs routine for protection." Jim replies," That is very sad Doc. Thank you for the update. Robin and I have to finish rounds and meet Captain Jake for a meeting before we finish up our twelve hour shifts. We have been covering vacations the past two weeks.” Robin waves as she and Jimmy push the cart to exit the infirmary and says,” Have a good day Docs! Nice to see you both.” Dr. Jay Sutton says,” I am heading to my office. I will meet you for lunch at the diner at noon.” He exit’s the infirmary door as I hear a loud familiar voice say,” Hey Doc J! How the hell have you been?” Dr. Sutton laughs aloud as he replies,” Living the dream my man! I have been very busy but all is well with me. Thanks for asking dude! Catch you on the flip side!” John enters the infirmary door laughing and says,” Hey my favorite Doc Mama! I know you missed me while I was gone!” Yeah, yeah son! I missed you like a plague. Take a seat and tell me how your trip to Cooks Forest, Pennsylvania went. We both laugh as we sit down at my desk. “I went on a 5 mile canoe trip down the river and stayed at Macbeth Cabins. The cabin sits on a hill with the creek running directly in the back. When the window is open, it sounds like it is raining. It has one large room with a bathroom and a shower stall. The radiator heater is located in between two full beds and the large porch has a fridge and stove. Danielle and I sat in the back of the cabin in front of an amazing campfire until we couldn’t stay awake any longer. Jake and April stayed in the cabin right next to ours.” he said with a smile. Didn’t you have to reserve the cabin a year in advance? “Yep.” he quipped. Your dad and I went up there for our honeymoon for a canoe trip and we planned on getting a motel room but we stopped in the general store to pick up a few things for the cooler which is right next to the office, We stopped in the office to pick up a brochure and asked the desk clerk how long in advance we needed to make a reservation. She said a year and they had no cabins available just then. The phone rang while we were standing there and luck would have it that a couple cancelled their reservation for the week beginning the very next day. We took the cabin for three days and thirty years ago, it was only sixty five dollars a night. Andy and I had the most relaxing time and slept like babies. "Wow! Try one hundred and fifty big ones a day now but so damn worth it! A hell of a lot better than a motel room any day! We stopped at the general store and cooked all week. We called to order a pizza and the only pizza joint in town wanted twenty bucks for six slices. No damn way we were desperate enough to pay that!" he said with a smirk. Well, sweet child of mine. Not! I laugh at the crooked smile John gives me. I have been here since four thirty so I am going home at noon. Pass on to the guard at the front gate that the funeral home will be here this evening at eight to pick up Inmate Amos Moses from the infirmary. I already told Warden Andrew and now you, to be at my house Friday at five for a cookout. I will stop by Jakes office and tell him on my way out in a few minutes. Dr. Sutton is bringing beer and informed me that he is looking forward to kicking all of your butts at corn hole. “Aw! Hell no he ain’t! My brothers and I will be stomping him into the ground!” he said with a laugh and an impish grin. Sounds like fun and I have to go my son. “I will walk you out Mama.” he said with a smile. Nurse Marthagail approaches my office door as I grab my bags to leave for the day. “Have a good day Doc. Lamar and I will be over Friday for your cookout. We will be whooping all you all in corn hole, especially you John,” she said with a smile. “Everybody’s a comedian!” John said with a laugh. The funeral home will be here this evening at eight to pick up Inmate Moses. The paper work is on my desk in an envelope. “I will pass that on to Nurse Bethany when she arrives at three.” she said.

Nurse Bethany arrives to the infirmary on time as usual while Nurse Marthagail finishes arranging the shelves in the cabinets above the carts. They walk into the office for report. “Hello Bethany. How are your beautiful kiddos doing?” asked Nurse Marthagail. Nurse Bethany replies with a radiant smile,” They are growing like bad weeds. Hayden started Kindergarten this year and Emilee just turned a year old last week.” Nurse Marthagail replies,” Rug rats grow up faster than you can blink. One day you put them on the bus for Kindergarten and before you know it. You are attending their high school graduation ceremony. I finished stocking the medication room and organized the cabinets. There is a tote in the medication room that has expired medications to be returned to the pharmacy with the next delivery in the morning. The envelope for the funeral home is right here on the desk. Stratton and Boroski will be here at eight to pick up Inmate Moses. Doc notified the main gate guard that they would be picking him up then as well." Nurse Bethany replies," Thank you Marthagail. You have a nice evening and be careful going home." After Marthagail leaves, she leaves the infirmary and takes the stairs located by the service elevator down to the morgue. She removes Inmate Amos Moses from the morgue drawer and retrieves the ventilator from the storage rooms hidden closet along with the duffle bag containing intubation tubing and extra supplies for the ventilator. Intubating him and attaching the ventilator his body temperature begins to rise. His heart beat is very faint and can only be heard with a stethoscope. A palpable pulse cannot be felt and his respirations on his own are only one breath per minute at this moment. The ventilator is oxygenating his body completely due to the tetrodotoxin beginning to wear off. She puts on a gown and gloves and unwraps the sterile towels containing the surgical instruments needed to extract both kidneys. The cooler containing dry ice was left in the bottom cabinet prior to going home this morning before Nurse Marthagail arrived at four A.M. Turning him into his left side to make an incision to the left flank area to extract the right kidney placing it in a bag and into the cooler. Closes the incision with fine sutures and then proceeds to turn him onto his right side to extract the left kidney in the same manner. Removes the ventilator and extubates Inmate Moses. Inspects his body and the metal table in which he is laying for any blood before covering him with a sheet and placing him back into the morgue fridge. The metal cart is on wheels that rolls into the fridge. There are two individual drawer compartments in which the metal tables pull out if needed. She cleans up the morgue and places the cooler back into the bottom cabinet to be picked up later. She hurries back up the stairs and stops at the break room vending machine for coffee. If she is seen by a guard she needs to be seen coming out of the break room and not from the basement. She returns to the infirmary and sits at the desk in the office. She takes a deep breath and sips her hot coffee. Thinking to herself," That is extremely hard work by myself. The money will be worth it but I can't stand the thought of getting caught. Claudia is going to be crucified when she gets caught. Ten thousand dollars a kidney, twenty thousand for a liver, thirty thousand for an entire lung and fifty thousand dollars for a heart. Too many people die everyday on waiting lists for organs. I am not going to feel guilty for helping good people live longer that actually deserve to." As Nurse Bethany waits for the funeral home transport van to pick up Inmate Amos Moses, she walks to the medication room to put away a few supplies that arrived after Nurse Marthagail went home. Guards Caroline Hurley and Dale Egbert arrive to the infirmary with an inmate slumped over and gasping for air in the wheelchair. Nurse Bethany hears them calling her name and comes out of the medication room as the guards are assisting him onto the cart. Guard Caroline says," As I was making rounds on cell block C, Inmate Paul Poulist was slumped over at the edge of his cot and gasping for air. I radioed Guard Dale to bring the wheelchair immediately." Nurse Bethany replies, " Thank you for getting him here quickly." She places the pulse ox on his finger to get an oxygen content reading which results at eighty six percent so she places him on oxygen at two liters via nasal cannula. Listens to his lungs and hears very faint air exchange throughout both lungs. She pulls up his medical record on the computer and finds a prn order for an aeresol treatment due to his history of asthma. She adds an ampule of medication to an aeresol mask and applies the mask to his face then turns the dial on the wall for air pressure. As she stands at the cart side to continue monitoring his breathing, he begins to relax with steady breathing. Guard Caroline places the shackle on his left wrist and left ankle and says," How is he doing Nurse Bethany?" " His pulse ox reading is ninety four percent and slowly increasing. I will be holding him here for twelve hours for observation per our Respiratory Protocol," she said. Guard Caroline replies," Guard Dale will be posted just outside the infirmary door for the night shift." "Ok and thanks again for bringing him down. You have a nice rest of your shift Guard Caroline and Guard Dale," Nurse Bethany said with a smile. Just as Guard Dale sits down outside the infirmary door, the desk phone in the office rings. The guard at the gate notified me that the funeral home transport van was passed through the gate to the back door of the morgue. She grabs the envelope from the desk and as she opens the infirmary door, Guard Dale is informed that she is going to the morgue to let the funeral home transport technicians in to release Inmate Amos Moses to them along with the authorization and release forms Dr. Jay Sutton signed. As she opens the morgue door, there are three technicians instead of two. She smiles as she introduces herself," Hello. I am Nurse Bethany and I have the forms you require." The tall slim technician with coal black hair and pale narrow face replies," Nice to meet you. I have a form for you to sign that gives us consent to pick up the deceased for our records." The other two technicians are tall with normal builds with blonde hair and tanned faces. They look like brothers. They load Inmate Moses on their cart and place a red velvet blanket over his entire body. The one technician opens the door and the other two push the cart out the door. As she walks through the morgue the door opens and the technician steps back into the morgue while the door closes behind him. He steps toward Nurse Bethany and extends his arms to hug her and says," I told the driver I forgot the personal belonging bag that is to accompany him to the funeral home." She replies," I placed the cooler in this black duffle bag for you to drop off at the clinic within the hour. That was a good idea getting a job at the funeral home. You will be able to pick up the organs I can collect without raising suspicion. You will be performing the body prep and embalming which is perfect. I knew I married you for a reason." she said as she laughs. Mike replies, " I will see you when you get home my lovely wife." He exit's the morgue with the duffle bag and Nurse Bethany leaves the morgue to the elevator to return to the infirmary. As she enters the infirmary she thinks with a smile," This job is perfect to continue our organ transfers for people that deserve them. Certainly not prisoners that have no right being alive. My mother, Nurse Claudia is the best nurse ever! She taught us all about the deserving people on organ donor waiting lists and all the lives we are saving." She approaches Doc Betty's office and says," Hey Doc! I met my husband for lunch and would like to know if there is anything you would like me to work on." You can take a look in the medication room and put away the supplies that arrived while you were on your lunch break. I will be leaving soon. I have to teach in the lab this evening. Thank you for asking. " Anytime Doc! That's what I am here for." she replied with a smile. No sooner as Dr. Betty Reaper leaves the prison Guards Jimmy and Robin arrive through the infirmary doors with a prisoner ina wheelchair clutching his chest and wincing. Guard Jimmy says," We have prisoner Brian Labbe for you! During rounds he was yelling from his cell. We grabbed him immediately because Doc will certainly have our asses if we don't treat our prisoners with respect and dignity." Nurse Bethany replies," Don't I know that! Place him on the cart and I will assess him. Thank you both." They secure his wrist and ankle with shackles as they warn him to be on his best behavior because he knows what the outcome will be. Bethany says," You both can leave now. I will let you know if he needs a sitter." They both exit the infirmary as she begins her assessment. His vital signs and symptoms currently, she initiates the chest pain protocol. She medicates him per protocol and as his chest pain subsides, vital signs stabilize and he is resting with his eyes closed, she charts all of the tests she performed along with an ekg and blood work, she has to call the lab for a pick up as well as send Doc a message to update her. She prints out the requisition for the lab and sends a message to Doc. As she sits at the desk to begin her charting, she evaluates Brian Labbe's complete medical history. With a smile on her face she thinks to herself, " This prisoner is perfect for involuntary organ donation. His blood type is universal O negative. I am sure I can send his extra blood work to Mike so he can type match the patients on the organ donor list," The desk phone rings and she answers," Hello Doc!" I am just calling for a quick update while my students are on a fifteen minute break. How is Brian Labbe doing? "He has been stable since he came in. I just performed his vital signs again per protocol and they are normal. He has been resting with no further complaints or any abnormal readings on the cardiac telemetry monitor." she replies happily. OK. Just let me know if there are any changes and I will see him in the morning. Thank you for letting me know Bethany. You have a nice shift. "Thanks Doc. You do the same." she replies. As she charts she thinks to herself," Mike is bringing me dinner as well as pick up the extra blood I drew for the type match he needs. I will be working the next two days awaiting the results to make my move. I sure hope he is a match1" As she gets up from the desk, her cell phone vibrates in her pocket. Bethany gets an immediate smile as she sees a text message from unknown. It reads, Hello my sweet daughter. You are missed and loved each and every moment I don't see you. I will keep in touch with burner phones as often as I can. Ray and I are moving around a lot which has worked for us so far. Tell my sweet granddaughter Emilee I miss and lover her so very much. I sent a few lines to Abbey and Dominique. Keep up the good work we have done for so many special people in need and please be very cautious. Love always, Mom. As she deletes the message with tears in her eyes she thinks about all the good they do and how she does not want to get caught and become a wanted fugitive as her Mom and Ray are. Emilee is only two years old in which she would suffer more than any of us. I will have to make this my last death with organ theft and just focus on being a nurse. I love being a nurse but love being a mother more. Her cell phone vibrates in her pocket once again. A text message from Mike that reads, Hi my beautiful wife! I am awaiting your appearance at the back morgue door with dinner. I love you more everyday. Love forever. Mike. She smiles as she callls the guards to watch Brian so she can meet Mike. Guard Jimmy arrives then she exit's the infirmary to the elevator to the basement and to the morgue. She opens the morgue s back door and Mike gives her the dinner bag as she hands him the blood stored in a cold cylinder. He gives her a quick kiss then closes the door. The door beeps as to secure the alarm status. An employee code is needed to open the door. She exit's the morgue to return to the infirmary. Guard Jimmy always has a sincere smile every time I see him. He is genuinely respectful and kind with every tone I see him encounter. He says" Your patient has been sleeping since you left. No alarms from the cardiac monitor." She replies," Thank you Jimmy. I appreciate you stopping up. Have a nie shift. I will call you again if I need your assistance." He waves as he exit's the infirmary. I will finish putting away supplies and assess Brian Labbe so I can finish his charting before Nurse Marthagail comes in. I sit at the desk to finish charting as Nurse Marthagail enters the infirmary with a smile and her southern charming accent says," Good morning my young friend! How are ya? I bet that beautiful youngen of yours is growing like a weed!" Nurse Bethany replies with a smile," She sure is! I am fine and thanks for asking. I enjoy being back to work here." " We are happy to have you back. Having an efficient nurse to work with is a definite pleasure around here sweety!," Nurse Marthagail replied. " I put all the supplies away in the medication room as well as organized everything. I will give you report when you are ready", said Bethany. "I will put my bag down and you can give me report so you can git home to that beautiful little sprout," Marthagail said with a big smile. Reort is given and Bethany picks up her bag and exit's the infirmary. Nurse Marthagail assess Brian and charts her normal findings. Blood work will be due in a few hours along with a repeat ekg then Doc Betty will arrive soon after that. I love working with that sweet amazing doctor! She makes a pot of coffee and hears the infirmary door open. "how is my beautiful wife doin this morning?" Lamar says. She replies," What the heck are you doin here so carly?" "I have a few early transport to court at seven a.m. I received the weekly schedule yesterday. Actually, I have ten early transport appointments to court this week," he replied. "well, well then. Coffee is almost done. Do you want a cup before you leave?", she asked. "Heck yes I do!" he replied with his southern accent that is more drawn than hers. She pours him a cup of coffee and adds cream and sugar, just the way he likes. He takes a few sips and applies the lid. He says" Goodbye my love! Have a good day!" He waves at Marthagail as he exit's the infirmary. Brian asks to get up and go to the restroom, so I call the guards on duty to remove his shackles and walk him to the restroom. Guards Will Drost and Carolyn Hurley arrive in a timely manner as always. Will waits outside the door and Carolyn says," Hey Nurse Marthagail! How are you nice lady! I havent seen you in quite some time! I usually work afternoon shift but I picked up several dayshift slots for Captain Jake." Marthagail replies," Well sweety, It is very nice to see you as well! I just work the same twelve hour shifts as I have for the last fifteen years here, You just missed Lamar," she says with a smirk and laugh. Carolyn replies,: OH! I just love that hilarious man! He could make a dog laugh! Everybody adores his sense of humor and jokes!" "Well! Try living with the man! I enjoy my time away from him but I agree with you. I have been married to him for fifty-four years!" she says with a loud laugh. Guard Will assists Brian back to the cart and applies the shackles to his left wrist and left ankle. I straighten up his sheet and blanket and perform his routine prorocol vital signs and ekg with blood work to follow. Guards Will and Carolyn say," Call us if you need anything." They wave as they exit the infirmary. I finish everything with Brian and sit at the desk to chart and enjoy a cuo of coffee in peace. I call the lab for a specimen pick up and as I hang up the phone I hear the infirmary door code and the door swings open as Doc walks in. "Hey Doc! Good morning! You are an early bird today!"

Marthagail says as she stands up to offer Doc Betty a seat. Thank you for the warm welcome my friend! It is always a brighter morning when I see you! "You always say the sweetest thangs my friend!" Marthagail replies with a smile. How is Lamar doing? I saw him putting gas in the transport van when I arrived. He doesn't usually arrive until eight a.m. "he was here earlier and I made coffe and sent a cup with him. He has several appointments at seven a.m. to court appearances. He said he had many early appointments all week." she said. I waved at him when I arrived, so I am sure he wil stop by later. I always enjoy seeing him. He really brightens my day when he visits and tells me a few jokes with that southern twang. Marthagail laughs and says," Yeah, yeah! I live with him and I know that for sure." You can give me report and I will assess him so I can chart my findings in his chart profile. We sit at my desk and drink coffe while report is given. Nurse Marthagail goes to the medication room to pull Brian's morning medications while I perform my assessment. How are you feeling Brian? He replies," I am feeling better Doc. I feel weak and still have nausea but no chest pain right now. I just feel achy all over." I will have Nurse Marthagail give you some Tylenol with your morning medications. I perform my assessment and my findings are within normal limits. The cardiac monitor is reading normal sinus rhythm. Ok Brian. Everything looks good. I will go to the medication room and ask Nurse Marthagail to give you some Tylenol. He replies, “Thank you Doc. You are the best!.” I proceed to the medication room and relay the Tylenol order to Marthagail. Back to my office and the desk phone rings. “ Good morning my amazing wife! Just wanted to let you know that I love you and I will be in Grayson most of the day in the Military recruiting office. I was asked to sit in with the recruiter to evaluate some potential Navy recruits. I will be home for dinner so I will have it ready for you when you get home.” Well thank you for calling my amazing husband. I will see you later. Have fun at the recruiting office. “I am actually looking forward to being there. See you later sweetheart.” he replied as he hung up. I proceed to Brian’s chart to update his profile as I see last looked at by Nurse Bethany Rutt. I wonder why she was looking at his main profile. I imagine she is just very precise with her patient care and wanted to be sure of his medical history which is a reasonable reason. I proceed to his lab work profile with everything being within normal ranges but still have this mornings lab work pending. My phone rings once again. “Hey Doc Mama! Just checking in with you! What have you been up to?” Captain Jake asks with a chipper voice. Hey my son! I am good. I always enjoy hearing from you!

What are you doing for dinner today? " Is that an invitation? I would love to have dinner with the greatest Mama in the world! April is free for dinner as well! I just spoke to her before she began rounds and she asked me what we were doing for dinner. She will be excited to have dinner with you and Michael!" he relied happily. Great! I will ask your brothers if they want to join us. Michael is cooking so I will send him a text message and give him heads up. " Wow! That sounds like a party during the week! I would like to see my brothers out from this place. I will bring dessert." he said with a deep laugh. Good my wonderful son! I will see you at six p.m. "See you all then Mama!I will stop by later to see you when I round." he replied. As I hang up the receiver the infirmary door opens and I hear a loud familiar voice say," Hey Doc G! I miss my Doc Grim Reaper!" he says with a grin as he enters my office. John! Oh! How I miss your sick sense of humor, Not! I laugh as I smile at my ornery youngest son. I just received a call from Jake. I invited him and April to dinner this evening at six p.m. Do you want to join us? "Hell yeah! I love having dinner with you and Michael and maybe my crazy brothers too!" laughing as he replied. I have to call Andrew and hope he can join us. I may have to pour on the charm if he is busy. "Naw! He will make time for me! I am his favorite! As a matter of fact, I am everybody's favorite!" he says while smiling his Cheshire cat grin. Yeah yeah you are my son! Not! You better keep dreaming my crazy son! I laugh with him. "I have to go finish rounds Doc G Mama! I will definitely see you for dinner. I will bring the beer!" he says as he leaves my office waving at the window as he exit's the infirmary. I pick up the phone and enter Warden Andrew's extension. He answers," Hey Mother! Nice to hear from you. How have you been?" Good my son! Nice to hear your kind stern voice. I just had the pleasure of visiting with your brother John and a phone call from your brother Jake. "Wow! What did you do to deserve their attention?" he laughs as he asked. I was told that I am the Greatest Mama in the world my son. I believe that is why I received their attention. He laughs with his deep voice and says," I totally agree with them my sweet mother Doc!" I am calling to ask if you would like to join us all for dinner this evening at six p.m.? Michael is cooking, Jake is bringing dessert and John boasted he was bring beer. Laughing he says, " I would love to join you all! I have been missing my wonderful family time away from here!" Jake said the exact same thing. "Great minds think alike though I am the smartest one of our bunch!" Yes you are and that stays between us my genius son. "Great mother! I will see you all later!" he said with a sincere voice. See you later my son. I return the receiver and the phone rings immediately. "

Hey my friend! I was wondering if you would like to take over my lecture at the medical school this evening?" asks Dr. Jay Sutton. I am sorry my friend. I have a dinner date with my entire family this evening at six p.m. I havent spent any time with them for quite a while so I am looking forward to seeing them all. Michael is cooking. He replies," No problem. I will call Doc Eva Dawn and ask her to cover me. Do you have an extra chair for your oldest friend?" Absolutely. I will send a message to Michael to add you to our dinner party. Excitedly he replies," Great! I will bring dessert and your favorite wine!" That is the best news I have heard in a while my old friend. See you later. "have a good day my friend. I will see you later. Bye!" he said with a laugh. I am really looking forward to dinner. My crazy funny family makes life so enjoyable. My family is a true gift from God. I need to put together a family cookout and invite my parents and my sisters. I will give Agent Alice Brubaker a call and invite her as well. I have enjoyed the time I have spent with her. We met for dinner and drinks twice last month. I will plan that for next wekkend. I will let everyone know this evening and call everyone else tomorrow. I pick up the receiver and call Agent Alice Brubaker. She answers immediately and says," Hello Doc! Nice to hear from you. How have you been?" I have been good Alice. I am calling to let you know that I am planning a family cookout next weekend and would like to invite you. She replies," I would love to attend your family cookout! Letting loose is exactly what I need! Spending time with your family on a non professional occasion is going to be great!" Oh! You have no idea how wild my family is my friend! "I could only imagine! I am a profiler Doc. I could read them pretty well. Especially John. I saw him in action when I was at the prison, I am surely right about him! I am looking forward to seeing Captain Jake and Warden Andrew in a laid back wild setting!," she said with a laugh. Yes. I am certain you have hit the head with my sons. I laugh with her. Saturday at two p.m. "That sounds great! I am so glad you called Doc!," she replied sincerely. Have a good day and I will see you next Saturday. "I wouldn't miss it for anything. See you then Doc! You have a good day!," she replied with a loud laugh. I will notify everybody tomorrow to save that date. I am so very lucky to have the family and friends in my life. I adore each and every one of them. I will ask Martagail and Lamar to join us. That will be free entertainment for sure! Look out Jerry Springer! You have nothing on these people! I chuckle to myself. I need to get my quarterly budgets together but first I am going to assess inmate Brian Labbe and chart in his profile. Hello Brian, how are you feeling? "I am feeling better Doc. The Tylenol worked for the body aches.," he replied kindly with a soft voice. Your blood work looks good I am expecting results soo from your lab work drawn this morning. Your twenty four hour observation will be up at six p.m. As long as you remain stable and your next lab work is within normal limits, you will be released back to your cell. "OK Doc. Thank you for your wonderful=l care as well as your staff. I appreciate everything you all have done for me." he replied kindly. You are very welcome Brian. I have some work to do in my office. Let Nurse Marthagail know if you need anything. "I will Doc." he replied. Back to my office to work on quarterly budget reports. I sent Michael a message for our big dinner party and he responded," I can cook for an army but Navy sounds better! Looking forward to seeing everybody as well. Love you always" I am going to be picked on profusely by my sons but I can handle them all. Laughing to myself as I type away number after number on my report. These days go by so fast. Nurse Bethany will be arriving in an hour. I finish the reports and as I email them to accounting department, Nurse Bethany Rutt walks into my office with a brilliant smile adns says," Hey Doc! It's always nice to see your sweet face!" You are so very kind my dear! Always nice to see you as well sweet girl My phone rings as I walk around my desk. I pick up the receiver and a familiar voice answers." Hello my friend! I was wondering if you could spare some time for a lunch date soon," asked Agent Alice Brubaker. I can set time aside for you anytime my friend. I am meeting with my family for a barbeque tomorrow. You are welcome to join us at 1600. "That sounds great Doc! I will be there! I will bring beer and my famous potato salad. See you tomorrow Doc! Thank you for the invite!", replied Agent Brubaker. Nurse Marthagail and Nurse Bethany are finishing with report and I will put everything away and exit this place until Monday. Nurse Marthagail asks," Doc, can I walk out with you?" I would love and escorted walk to my vehicle my friend! Nurse Bethany proceeds to assess Inmate Brian. "Hello Brian! How are you feeling?" asked Nurse Bethany. "Hello to you Nurse! I am still feeling weak and actually nauseated currently," said Inmate Brian. " You will be observed here until tomorrow morning. Doc kept you an extra day to monitor your vital signs. Your blood pressure reading is low. I can insert an IV and run some IV fluids to bring your blood pressure up. The extra fluids will make you feel better as your blood pressure increases. I can give you some medication through your IV for nausea as well," verbalized Nurse Bethany. "Thank you so much Nurse for being so kind and caring. You know I am here because my brother robbed a bank as I was waiting in the car. I had no idea what he was doing! I was charged as an accomplice and second degree murder. He shot and killed the security guard because he rushed my brother Willie Lee," he said with teras in his eyes. "I am so very sorry Brian! That happens a lot more than I care to think about honestly! I am going to the medication room and I will be back to administer the IV and you medication," she said with a smile. Guards Jimmy and Robin walk into the infirmary to relieve Guard Will Droste. "Hey mister bad ass!," says Guard Jimmy. Guard Robin replies," OH Really Jim! You know Will was just doing his job! Though I have to agree with Jim! Taking down three prisoners during a riot in the mess hall by yourself was pretty Bad Ass I have to admit!" she says with a grin. Will replies," Thank you for that! Captain Jake was impressed. It takes an amazing effort to impress him! He has accomplished so much towards his careers. He did tell me I did a very professional take down without injury to any prisoner," he replied with a half smile. "Goodbye Guard Bad Ass!" says Guard Jimmy as the wave and Guard Will exit's the infirmary. Guard Robin asks ,"Hi Brian. How are you feeling today?" As he replies nurse Bethany arrives at the bedside with his medications," I am still weak and sick to my stomach but Nurse Bethany is going to fix me up. Thank you for asking Guard Robin. "Ok people! Guard Jimmy could you please move your chair near Guard Robin so I can work please ?asked Nurse Bethany. " absolutely Ma'am! " replied Guard Jimmy with an impish grin. As Nurse Bethany finishes inserting the IV catheter and runs the IV fluids through an IVAC system, pushes the nausea medication through his IV tubing Inmate Brian begins to close his eyes and rests comfortably at this time. " I have to go to the office and get some charting done on Inmate Brian," says Nurse Bethany. Guards Jimmy and Robin wave at her with smiles. I made it home and get a shower before dinner. I am going to make some side dishes for the barbeque tomorrow and I am so excited to see my crazy funny family along with Dr. Jay Sutton, whom I met in college and attended medical school with is a very precious friend as well as colleague. Agent Alice Brubaker whom I had the pleasure to work with on Nurse Claudia's case which is still open. She is a very good friend that I have become very close with. I have spaghetti on the stove for dinner as I cool macaroni pasta for macaroni salad. I am going to make my famous Cheesy potatoes with the crushed cornflake topping that my entire family loves. Mike walks into the kitchen and hugs me so snuggly it feels like he may crush me and says," Hello my beautiful doctor wife! How was your day? I see you are prepping for our barbeque. I put away all of the steaks and hamburger as well as the hotdogs in the fridge in the garage as I came in. I can't tell you enough how much I adore you and your sons! You are the lihjt that guides me back to you!" You are so dramatic Admiral! I am blessed to have you in my life my dear husband! Now go away so I can finish dinner and the food for tomorrow! I laugh at him as he bows and replies," Yes your majesty1 My Queen!" I wave him out of the kitchen as I giggle to myself He is so dramatic sometimes but has a heart of gold. He never fails to tell everyone he cares for that he loves them. I have witnessed him on his ship with the sailors and he is very stern and professional. I have never heard anything but respectful words as I exit the ship when the sailors are gathered in the halls of the ship. As I finish cleaning the kitchen, I pour a very much needed glass of Merlot and sit in my favorite reclining chair by the gas fireplace and pick up my third book in a series that I have to finish so I can purchase the next series that just came out by my favorite author Nora Roberts. I like Julie Garwood as well. I will read or reread several of her books as soon as I finish Nora Roberts. My phone rings as I take a big gulp of my wine. Hello Nurse Bethany! How are you this evening? She replies," I am sorry to bother you Doc! Inmate Brian's blood pressure was very low at the beginning of my shift, so per protocol I inserted an IV and administered a liter of IV fluids as well as administering nausea medication. He only complained of feeling weak and nauseated. His blood pressure then remained low. I left his side for a few miutes to grab another bag of IV fluids and Guards Jimmy and Robin yelled for me to come quick, Guard Robin started CPR and Guard Jimmy asked if he should call an ambulance. I assisted Guard Robin with CPR and applied the defibrillator patches. Jimmy called the squad as I pushed medication through his IV and got the reading to push the button to advise shock. The ambulance arrived and we were unable to revive Inmate Brian." she said with a grief stricken voice. Oh! that is so very sad! I will call Dr. Jay Sutton to evaluate Brian and I will ask him if he wants me to assist him, but I hope he turns me down this time. I have been cooking since I came home for our barbeque tomorrow. I am sure you did everything you could honey. I will call him now. she replies," Thanks Doc! I needed your reassurance. You are truly an amazing boss! Have fun tomorrow Doc!" Thank you honey. I call Dr. Jay and he answers," Hey my gorgeous friend! What's up?", he says with that charming deep voice. There was a sudden death in the infirmary my friend. Inmate Brian just expired. When you arrive< Nurse Bethany will give you report as well as have your paperwork on my desk. he replies," Thanks for the notification my friend. I will see you tomorrow for the entertaining barbeque!" As we hang up, I let out a deep breath that he didn't ask me to assist him this evening. I a, exhausted from the entire week and cooking for tomorrows better than Jerry Springer entertainment. I will call my parents and Mike's family to join us. Wow! Now that will be a true day of laughter that will make your ribs hurt from laughing so much! My mother is Nurse Marthagail and my father is the one and only, prisoner transport driver, Lamar! He is true character of comical entertainment. My sister, Guards Carolyn Hurley and Jake's wife, Guard April Sigler. Mike's family, retired Judge, Nancy Consiglia, his brothers, Anthony and Todd Tedesca as well as sister in law, Chrissy Tedesca. Shelley Tedesca is the prison administrator and her son Connor is in Law school. Nurse Bethany scurries to get rid of her syringe of Tetrodotoxin. She called her husband Mike to be prepared to pick up organs as soon as Dr. Jay Sutton finishes his evaluation and signs off on the death certificate. Dr. Jay Sutton enters the infirmary and begins his thorough assessment. An hour later he hands Nurse Bethany the paperwork and approves the transfer to the chosen funeral parlor which is Staton Baroski that's 5 miles away. Nurse Bethany calls Guards Carolyn Hurley and Guard April Sigler to transport Inmate Brian to the morgue. Nurse Bethany hurries to the morgue to begin surgical extraction of Inmate Brian's kidneys, heart and liver along with the pancreas. Mike told her the Organ Life Banc has a patient on the list now waiting for kidneys and a pancreas. A patient awaiting a heart as well as a liver. All the prisoners at this facility volunteered to be typed and tested for organ donation. Mike has all of the information that Nurse Claudia provided while she was employed here. Bone marrow is a need all across the world. Nurse Bethany puts Inmate Brian on a ventilator and begins her prep. As she places the organs in surgical sealed bags and places them in separate coolers containing dry ice. Inmate Brian 's incisions sutured with expert precision. She removes the ventilator tubing and places it back in the closet. She whispers in Brian's ear ," I am sorry Brian but your organs were in need to save innocent people's lives. It was very sad for your incarceration but you are saving three good people in which one of them is just a teenager.. His life is quickly fading from the Tetrodotoxin. She places a pillow over his face an he quickly fades away. Mike knocks on the back bay delivery door. She opens the door and he quickly picks up the coolers and kisses Nurse Bethany before exiting the back door. Loads the van and leaves as fast as he arrived. Nurse Bethany places his body into the morgue cooler and cleans up her mess so she can return to the infirmary to clean Brian's cart and bay area. She has to chart everything thoroughly for his permanent records.

She just finishes and calls the funeral parlor to pick him up. He had no other family to notify as is brother was sent to a different prison that has maximum security in Ohio. Nurse Marthagail arrives through the infirmary door with most precise timing. Nurse Bethany sighs with relief that she was able to finish everything in time to leave promptly. Nurse Marthagail enters the office and says," Well Bethany! How was your night? I see Inmate Brian was sent back to his cell……" As Bethany gives her furrowed eyebrows. .Nurse Bethany replies, "No…He expired at midnight. He suddenly began to decline. He crashed and had no vtal signs. Guards Jimmy and Robin assisted we tried to save him but when the ambulance arrived he expired.. I called the funeral parlor and they will be here at 0600 to pick his body up. I called Doc and updated her on everything as well." "Good night my sweet girl! Go home and get some rest and please give your beautiful babygirl Emilee Grace a kiss for me." Nurse Marthagail said with her brilliant smile and southern charm. As Bethany exit's the infirmary for the last time…..Lamar the prison transport driver arrives to the infirmary and says," Hey my beautiful southern bell! I brought you breakfast from the diner across the street. Bacon egg and cheese biscuits, hash browns and coffee," He says with his southern drawl which is soothing and charming. Nurse Marthagail gives

him her brilliant smile and replies with her southern drawl that isn't as prominent as Lamar's ," Thank you my husband. That was very sweet of you. Don't you have transports to get ready for? We have to go to Betty's barbeque today at 1700. "
"Yep! I surely remember we git to see our beautiful daughter, grandkids and especially that pecker head Mike!," he laughs with that deep belly laugh that is contagious. "Ok, Ok! Go on now so I can git my work started dear!' she sais with a stern voice. I awake at 0700 which is the longest I have slept in a very long time. I make coffee and boil some eggs for breakfast. Canadian bacon and wheat toast will be perfect. I have some strawberries in the fridge. Mike is outside setting up tables and chairs. The fire pit and the Corn Hole game.
The barbeque grill is set up and ready as well. We have coolers in the garage to fill with ice which will be full of beer after my sons arrive. This is going to be a great day! I love my family to the moon and back! My friends top off the family list! John will arrive back in town from his two week vacation in Hawaii. He consults with the Honolulu Police Department once in a while with his military background in the Navy Seals. That's why he has that arrogant and hilarious personality. I love it but I will never tell him that. His head is big enough! I begin to laugh as I think about how much I am going to enjoy this special day! I finish breakfast

and leave Mike's in the microwave. I have to shower and get dressed. I finish and sit in my favorite recliner with a second cup of coffee and pick up my Nora Robert book that I have to finish. Hours go by with peace and quiet as I read the final page of yet another amazing series! Now I can begin her next series with excitement and joy. She is truly a talented writer that really knows how to grab your interest with each page that just get better and better with intrigue and passion! I will begin reading her next series Monday evening when I get home from work. I straighten up the house and set out all of the disposable plates and cups as well as napkins and plastic silverware. The citronella candles and tiki torches are set up. Getting close to 1500 so Mike is heating up the grill already. I get more and more excited to see my family the closer it gets to 1700. My boys always arrive early to help set up. I am contemplating to record this shindig which could get one million hits on the internet in minutes! John is the first to arrive and says as his hands are raised," The main entertainment has arrived! He is laughing as he hugs and kisses me. Hi Momma! I missed you my sweet mother! You know I am your all time favoriye son! My brothers don't compare to me!" OH! get a grip you arrogant child of mine! I laugh as I ask him about Hawaii. "Hawaii was awesome Momma! I am considering moving there. I was offered a job on the Honolulu

Police Department as a sergeant. My navy Seal training is highly accepted and admired by them." That is amazing my sweet crazy son! You do what will make you happy honey. We will all come visit you! As I hug him and kiss him the back door swings open as Jake and April enter. Jake has his hands up as he says, " The King and Queen has arrived! The most amazing Man on earth has just arrived!" He and April hug and kiss me as the door swings open again. Andrew arrives with Carolyn Hurley whom is my baby sister. Will Droste follows right behind. He and Jake have been friends since eleventh grade technical school. Will hugs and kisses me as he says," Hi Momma! You know I am your favorite"! He laughs as he is hugging me tightly.. Listen up boy's and girl's! You are all my favorite people on earth so stop your arrogant behavior before I whoop you all! I laugh with them all as we all go outside so they can torment Mike. John yells towards Mike," Hey Mike! Do you want the master chef to cook on the grill for you?" Jake chimes in," I am the master chef of all time people so remember that! Laughing, Andrew says," You all are full of shit! I am the master of everything!" Good Lord! My sons are so full of themselves. As we all sit down, Marthagail and Lamar arrive, my sweet and crazy parents. John yells out," Oh no! Granny and Pap are here! Now let the party begin!" Dr. Jay and

Agent Alice arrive at the same time and caught the yelp of John as Agent Alice says," The real Boss has arrived so you all best behaveor I will whoop you all all by my lonesome!" Laughing, John yells," I am scared of you Alice! Not!" Dr. Jay chimes in and says," I will be more than happy to sit and observe all of the whooping about to occur!" We all are laughing with tears already. Jimmy and Robin arrive just in time for Jimmy to say,"I am the Mega Man out of you all! If anybody is going to deliver ass whooping time, that will be me to deliver!" All the boys say simultaneously, " OH! You couldn't fight your way out of a wet paer bag with holes in it!" Everyone is holding there stomachs from laughter and Lamar's laugh carries so we all laugh harder. Marthagail whispers to me," Nurse Bethany didn't show up to relieve me this morning. I had to call the agency to fill her slot. That isn't like her honestly. Maybe Inmate Brian's death put her over the edge." I don't belive that for a second! She is tough as they come! Something else is up! She replies," The funeral home picked up Brian at 0600. Steve is so sweet!" Just as I got up from the table to get a drink from the cooler the grill is full of food and almost done. My phone rings, "Sorry to bother you at home Doc! This is Steve from Staton and Baroski. The body we picked up this morning is, well… missing organs. The heart, kidney's and pancreas as well as the liver. During my cursory examination, He had precise incisions over each area the organs were removed. We X-rayed him and saw the evidence. I am aware Nurse Claudia and her husband Ray are at large but who would continue Nurse Claudia's work!," Nurse Bethany was on duty and didn't show up for duty this morning. I imagine she will be susoect number one right now. Agent Alice Brubaker is here as well as Dr. Jay Sutton. Since Nurse Claudia, we have been teamed up with her and the FBI until Nurse Claudia's case is closed and she is incarcerated for life! I will speak to them and we will come to you to have his body transferred to the county morgue with Dr. Jay Sutton which this is surely another murder case. Thank you for calling me Steve. You can call me anytime. "Thank you Doc. See you soon." he replied. I ask Dr. Jay and Agent Alice to follow me into the kitchen. I have some news for you both and you are going to be shocked! Inmate Brian expired yesterday at midnight. Dr. Jay evaluated him and signed his death certificate. His body was transferred to the funeral parlor at 0600. Steve just called me and informed me of the cursory exam. Incisions were above each organ that is missing which means murder. Agent Alice gasps and says,' You have got to be kidding me! Nurse Claudia has another accomplice! Nurse Bethany was on duty and a no show this morning, as I heard Marthagaial inform you. Sorry Doc, I read lips." Dr. Jay replies," I am so shocked! Sweet Nurse Bethany! Ok! We will all go to the funeral parlor in the morning and begin adding Bethany to the manhunt along with Nurse Claudia and Ray. We all return to the party and make plates to enjoy all of this wonderful food and family. We all finish eating and sit around the fight as the boys and girls fight, argue and laugh while playing corn hole. We light the Tiki torches and citronella candles. Conversation and continued laughter. My ribs are so sore from laughing so much. I had to wash my face from the mascara running from my eyes from happy tears and laughter of course. We all clean up from this glorious party while Mike is sitting by the fire pit with a beer in his hand and his eyes closed. He started setting everything up at 0600. he gets a reprieve from clean up this time as I laugh. I get in line for all the good by hugs and kisses from my wonderful family. My sweet and loving parenst whom gave me and my sisters the most amzing childhood. My parents hugged and kissed us everyday. still do! We had a magical and innocent childhood. Carolyn isn't my only sister….Sunday morning arrives too quickly honestly. As I make coffee, my phone rings," Hey Doc! Good morning my friend. I can't tell you how much I enjoyed your amazing family! Do yu have a time when you want to meet at the funeral parlor?" Dr. Jay wants to meet at 0900 if that's ok with you my friend. "That is perfect my friend! See you then," she says with a chipper voice. Too chipper for me this early. I have to drink at least three cups of coffee to even begin to feel chipper. I laugh at myself really. I do that often. Oh well, I will get dressed and venture over to the funeral parlor. We all arrive at the same time to the funeral parlor. Steve welcomes us as he takes us to Brian's body. As I examine his body along with Dr. Jay, Agent Alice Brubaker watches carefully. This is trly unbelievable! Agent Alice says," I did an extensive background check on Bethany Rutt as well as her husband Michael Rutt. Bethany is Claudia's daughter. I found her birth certificate from Ohio as well as Claudia's and Ray's. Michael Rutt is from Ohio as well." Dr. Jay and I look at each other with open mouthed shock and disdain. The prison did a background check on her when she was hired. I think the prison needs to use the FBI for new hire background checks for now on. Dr. Jay says'" Not a whole hell of a lot shocks me, but I am truly shocked.!" Agent Alice replies," We sent agents to Bethany and Mike's home which was found empty. They found a burner phone in a heating duct in the bedroom. They are analyzing it now. Hopefully we can find the whereabouts of Claudia, Ray as well as Bethany and Ray. Agents visited her daughters Abbigail and Dominique and their home was completely empty.

We are looking at all passports used and all transportation leading out of the state or country. I am sure we will get a hit. Someone in that damn family has had to make a few mistakes for us to find them all. I am certain they are all together hiding somewhere!" As the morgue assistants arrive to pick up Brian Labb, we assit them in loading Brian and then proceed to the morgue for a full forensic autopsy. We arrive at the morgue and begin the autopsy. Agent Alice's phone rings. "Are you serious! You got a hit on a credit card used for a rental car to be returned in Canada? Abbigail and Dominique? That is terrific! We alos got a hit on the burner phone. The last call was to Ontario Canada. We contacted the Canadian Mounties and they are on board to assist. The US Marshalls are on board as well.. Thank you for the excellent news and work you all have done! I will be returning to the office to gear up within the hour." That is the best news I have heard in a long time Alice! I would like to assist you if I could. "I would be honored to have you by my side Doc! I have been trying to get you to work with me and maybe this will be your final decision to approve the FBI's offer to you. You would be my partner ya know!," she said with a smile. I will call Mike and the infirmary to notify them. I have to make arrangements with the agency to send nurses all week until I return. I will go home to pack and I will meet you at your office. I arrive at Agent Alice's office and we begin to load up on a Leer jet headed for Ontario Canada. The Canadian Mounties call agent Alice Brubaker as she answers, Hi this is Mountie Rebecca Coy. We have apprehended your fugitives, Claudia and Ray Kirsh as well as her family. Abbigail and Dominique as well as Bethany and Michael Rutt with their toddler daughter Emilee Grace and their son Hayden Rutt. Ray's sons Tristan and Trenton own a home on the lake in Ontario along with a Yacht. They own a car dealership where Claudia and Ray were working to earn money while on the run. We will be expecting you all soon. "Thank you so very much Canadian Mountie Rebecca Coy! That is the best news ever!", Alice expressed with great joy. Well! Looks like you all can finally close your case against Claudia and her family. I have to admit that this is pretty exciting. I could get used to this Leer jet first of all. Agent Alice laughs and I laugh along with her. Agent Alice, there is something I have to inform you with. Please don't hold this information against me. "What is is Doc! I could never have any hard feelings against you my friend." she said with concern. OK, well, Claudia is my other sister I spoke about at my barbeque. I said I had sisters……

Made in the USA
Columbia, SC
24 April 2024

9e914c8a-ac2d-44aa-bd4a-d72f2a8961e1R01